GW00481884

The Sword Of Ralaira.

By J. P. Perry.

# The Sword of Ralaira.

Amazon Kindle Direct Publishing
https://kdp.amazon.com/en_US/
AmazonKDP

This edition self published by J.P.Perry 2018-07-11
First Published in Great Britain in 2018-07-11

ISBN 9781549567124

Illustrations by Scott Greenwood
Cover by Louis Greatorex
Image from iStock Photos

Imprint: Independently published

# The Sword of Ralaira.

The Sword of Ralaira.

The Sword of Ralaira.

For Charlotte

The best is yet to come.

# THE SWORD OF RALAIRA.

The Sword of Ralaira.

Chapter 1

Twins

Many years ago there lived a young man named Arion, and his sister, Francesca. They were twins. They both had blonde curls on their heads, and they both had the same shade of brown in their eyes. Francesca was said to be the most beautiful woman in all the land, and she most certainly was. Her hair fell in curls to her shoulders, beautiful gold, and her smile was warm and friendly.
They lived in the village of Comfort, named so as there certainly was lots of comfort in

all corners of this land. The houses, though small looking from the outside, opened wide on the inside. There was plenty of room for all of Arion's and Francesca's things, and then even more room for their comfy chairs and beds. This had been their home since they could remember, and they had never ventured very far from it. They did not need to. They had their house, and they had each other; and that was all they wanted.

A gentle stream ran by their house, home to kingfishers and goldfinches and dragonflies. The sound of running water could be heard throughout the house, as could the sound of the church bell ringing from across the hills.

The village of Comfort was tucked safely against the foot of a huge line of mountains, which stretched across the entire land. Here the town had hardly any wind, and was never bothered by the outside world.

Beyond the outskirts of Comfort, Arion and Francesca had no interest.

Every single morning, Arion made two cups of tea, one for him and one for his sister. They drank them together before setting off for work in the fields. The twins enjoyed their little talks in the mornings, and even discussed whether it was their favourite time of day.

*As the author of this book, I must apologise to you, the reader. I often get so carried away with descriptions and plots that I forget what I should be talking about. I have a feeling I will apologise a lot throughout our adventure.*
*I was meant to be describing the mountains, so I shall pick up from where I drifted off.*
The mountains around the town of Comfort were magnificent, like pillars stretching high to heaven, they made the people in Comfort feel very small, but they had grown accustomed to this. *With this in mind, however, I must say the villagers and town's folk often admired the mountains, and found them quite beautiful.*
In the morning, the sunbeams burst over them and lit the far forests alight. Francesca often woke up early just to see this, and sat in her front garden breathing

in the fresh air while reading her book, waiting for the sunrise.

Arion on the other hand, was not so keen to awaken so early, he thought that it was silly and often said 'Leave me alone, Francesca. Go and watch your sunrise.' for love each other as they did, they often had arguments, like brothers and sisters do. However, when the sun had gone from the sky and the stars shone above them, the twins never argued. Instead, they would sit and watch the beautiful night sky, and count the shooting stars. They counted to five, and whoever reached five first could make a wish. The twins often played this game, and felt most relaxed when they did so.

One night, Francesca reached five shooting stars first, and closed her eyes to make a wish.

'Make it a good one!' Arion laughed, still looking up to the sky.

Francesca thought about what she could wish for, she knew that she would always be happy here, and so was unsure about what to wish for. Then an idea then popped into her head from out of nowhere, the idea of an adventure for her and her brother.

Francesca had hardly ever thought about having an adventure before, but whenever she read about them in her books she did find them terribly exciting. And so, not knowing what else to wish for, she wished for an adventure.

Little did she know, but Francesca had set about a chain of events that would take the twins on an adventure that would determine the course of history. She never thought about that wish again, and so never realised that it was herself that had brought upon them the events of this book.

Francesca's wish would soon come true.

A good five miles away from Comfort, there lay the smaller town of Rundin. Not as nice as Comfort, but the villagers were on good terms with each other and often traded and had many dealings. Though again none of this bothered the twins, they stuck to their tiny farm, day in and day out, and that's how they liked it.

Rundin had become quite a trade route for people crossing through the lands and crossing back.  Its fancy beer and food would sell in bulk to those who wanted provisions to travel through Comfort. However, Rundin was not so safely tucked away into the mountainside as Comfort, and was much closer to the goings on of the bigger world, *as you will soon find out.*

*But our adventure starts when Arion and Francesca were on their way home after a hard days work down at their little farm. They slowly made their way up the hill to where their little house stood, taking in the last rays of the warm sun. Ready to go to bed.*

When they reached their front door, however, they discovered it was already open. Arion turned and asked if his sister had left it open that morning, she whispered back; 'I didn't, Arion. Someone must have broken in.'

The twins slowly crept through the door and into the living room. To their horror there sat a man in Arion's armchair. A huge man with a stubbly beard, a great long cloak wrapped around him, and a pipe that he was smoking quite cheerfully.

'Good afternoon.' said the stranger, looking gleefully at the two astonished faces standing in the doorway.

'Excuse me?' perked up Arion, trying to sound brave.

'Excuse you indeed,' piped back the stranger. 'Excuse you I will, but the question is do you excuse yourself?'

Arion was so shocked that he did not know how to reply to this madman, so he simply repeated.

'Excuse me?'

'Apology accepted my fine fellow, now make yourself useful and put the kettle on. You must be parched after your hard day's work.'

The two twins remained in the doorway, astonished.

It was at this moment that Francesca noticed that the man had the most brilliant green eyes, unlike anything she had ever seen before, they were almost shining. *There is a very important reason for the man's strange shade of eye colour, but you shall have to read on to find out what that reason is.*

Francesca finally stepped in front of her brother and asked the following question. 'Who on earth are you?' she screeched, for Francesca was easily stressed, as anyone would be finding this strangest of strangers in their living room.

'I am many things, but my name is Elrier, and yours is Francesca, is it not?'

'How do you know my name?' she asked.

'Ah, so I was right, thank you. Now Francesca, Arion, come inside and shut the door, I feel a draft and we have much to discuss.'

Without realising what they were doing, the twins had closed the door and followed the stranger into the kitchen, where he started to help himself to cheese, ham and bread from their stock.

This made the twins furious.

'Sorry, but who are you?' they both blurted out together.

'I have already said, I am Elrier, don't you people listen?'

'Yes we do!' answered Arion. 'But we also find it very rude of strangers to come into our house, uninvited! To start helping himself to our things!' he finished.

Elrier remained oblivious to this outburst and continued adding to the pile of food now clustered in his arms, humming merrily as he did so.

'Just stop!' screamed Francesca, and Elrier was instantly still. 'Let's start from the beginning. Why are you here? Why are you stealing our food?' she said.

'Not stealing my dear, packing. You shall see why. I will put these provisions here on this small table so you shall not forget.'

'Forget what?' shouted both the twins. *As you will see, Arion and Francesca often speak at the same time. No one really knows why, perhaps it's just because they're twins.*

'Never you mind.' Elrier said, even though it was their food. 'Now, you must listen carefully. Very soon, there will be a very important gathering. And it is of the upmost importance I feel, that you both must attend. I don't know why, but I feel it in my bones.'

'A gathering?' they asked again as Elrier moved across the kitchen and helped himself to a chair.

'Yes.' he said. 'A gathering. A once in a lifetime opportunity apparently. Your appearance is vital, I think.'

*What the twins did not know at this point was that this stranger, was a wizard. And an extremely powerful one. He was the Elrier, and seemed to be taking an interest in our two farm hands. Of course, I know why, but you shall have to keep reading, to tell you would ruin everything.*

Elrier ignored these questions and simply stared at the twins until Arion finally spoke.

'Alright, now I understand. This is my cousin Charlie isn't it, playing tricks?' he stated, trying to sound sure of himself.

'I assure you no tricks are playing here, young man.' replied Elrier. 'But if you want, I would be glad to show you an illusion or two.' he said chuckling and standing up. Arion had had enough, he pushed passed his sister and started to shuffle the man towards the door while he still chuckled on.

'Very funny, very good.' Arion said as he opened the door. 'Tell Charlie he got me, good day to you, sir.' he blurted as he shut the door behind the stranger.

With booming laughter sounding outside the house, Arion turned towards his sister, who was still just as startled as he was.

On most nights the twins would cook their food, take a walk and then bid each other good night. But on this night there was the obvious subject of the stranger in their house that both twins seemed to be ignoring. Plus the fact that the pile of food the stranger had been packing was indeed gone. But the stranger left empty handed, Arion had made sure. The pile of food on the small table however, had indeed vanished!

Arion spoke to his cousin soon after- (who lived but a mile down the road, the closest house) about the stranger in his house, and repeatedly asked Charlie why he had sent him. After many days of asking and asking, Arion gave up, and decided that the only explanation was that the stranger was indeed after the food. But must have hidden it all very well under his cloaks as he left the house.

Exactly a month later, there had been no sight of the stranger, the food, or of a 'once in a lifetime gathering.'

The twins had started to forget all about their little mishap, life was back to normal. But then as Francesca worked hard on the farm, she heard the town crier coming up their little stone road, shouting about something that chilled her to the bone.

'News friends! News friends! Great numbers gather at the town hall of Rundin tomorrow at dawn for a once in a life time opportunity. Vampires! Vampires in the flesh. Vampires in chains set to death tomorrow at dawn, watch em' swing!' he finally spat out.

Francesca suddenly remembered the words of that deranged stranger who was in her house stealing her bread.

'Gathering.' he had said. 'Once in a lifetime opportunity.' he had said.

She dropped her spade and ran as fast as her legs could carry her across to the next field where Arion was working.

'Francesca?' he said 'What is it?'

'It's all true, Arion. That crazy man in our house was right. I heard the town crier say it himself! A once in a lifetime chance.' she exclaimed.

'What? That's not possible, he was insane, it's all just a trick of some sort, Francesca.' he answered, and then he carried on with his work.

'No, Arion. There's something going on in Rundin, and I think we need to go and see what it is.'

'Francesca, you're being foolish, it's a days journey to Rundin, that's at least three days away from the farm. Who's going to make our money?' he asked.

'Fine.' she said. 'I can go on my own, I want to know what's going on even if you can't be bothered.'

This was new to Arion, she had hardly spoken in this manner before, and she seemed different. Usually she was happy to ignore the world outside of Comfort, but now she was already making her way down the road that led to Rundin.

Arion rushed to keep up behind her, bewildered at the fact that she was running away pointlessly.

'Francesca!' he sputtered. 'We are Fitley's, of Comfort.' *(Fitley was their second name, so you know.)*

'Arion Fitley needs no once in a life time opportunity, no running away into the big world and I'm surprised that his sister is showing any interest in....'

'Vampires!' she screeched with excitement. 'Imagine it, Arion. Real Vampires right in front of you. Now there's something you don't see everyday.'

'Vampires?' he hissed 'You mean the dangerous monsters with huge fangs and claws?'

'Arion, it's perfectly safe. They're in captivity. I want to see.' with that she started hurrying down the road away from her brother.

'I'll just stay here then... Do the dusting. It's fine.' he mumbled after her. The more he thought about it however; the thought of seeing actual, real vampires did seem exciting. He pondered over this thought as his sister journeyed further down the road. Could he follow her? Should he?

No he thought firmly, this was the only place for him and no amount of vampires or fairies or magical creatures could tear him away from it. His sister would return he thought, when she realised how silly all of this was.

He made his way home after that, slowly and calmly as always. That is, until he reached his door, where he turned abruptly and slammed it shut behind him. He shuffled into the living room and relaxed into his huge armchair. *As you will see throughout this book, Arion is a stubborn boy and now that he has made the decision not to see the vampires, he will be determined to stick to it.*

However, as he toddled into the kitchen, he suddenly remembered what the stranger had said 'A gathering...must attend...I'll put this pile of food over here on this small table so that you don't forget.' and with that, Arion turned to see the pile of food sitting on the table, as if it hadn't moved since the stranger had put it there. A surge of excitement bubbled in Arion's stomach and all of a sudden he realised that the stranger must have been magic. Elrier had hidden the food for when the time was right. Arion thought that maybe the stranger had been a wizard! All Arion wanted to do was charge after his sister, and go and see some real vampires!

Grabbing his jacket, his walking stick, the food from the table and his wallet full of pennies, Arion burst out of the door.

He turned and made sure it was locked and that all the lights were out. Then he ran down the stone path to find his sister. The twin's adventure had begun.

# Chapter 2

## The Mark of the Vampires.

It didn't take long for Arion to catch up with his sister, in fact she was so confident that he would give in to temptation, that she sat waiting for him over the hill. Although Arion was nervous about where they were going, there was nothing he enjoyed more than exploring the woods and fields that surrounded him. Everyday there was something new, something different.

Francesca took a deep breath, letting the cool, fresh air fill her lungs. She closed her eyes and listened to the sounds all around her, the faint and gentle wind, the rustle of the leaves and the musical songs of the birds.

'I knew you would come with me!' she teased.

Arion huffed and looked away, trying fiercely to hide the smile that had spread across his face.

\*\*\*\*

The village of Rundin was very different from what the twins were used to. The wind was much more powerful here, the houses were all extremely close together and the people were very shy and reserved.

At the head of the village, there stood a huge town hall, Arion thought it must have been the one of the biggest buildings he had ever seen!

Its huge oak doors were wide open, showing the gigantic hall inside. Rich tapestries lined every inch of the walls and from the ceilings dangled hundreds of lit candles, drowning the room in light that leaked outside through the doors, illuminating the street where Arion and Francesca stood.

Just to the left of the oak doors, there stood the dreaded gallows, where two nooses swung gently in the wind.

As the twins made their way closer, a crowd had started to gather. Men, women and children had all come to witness what was about to happen.

From behind the hall, guards dragged out two figures with swords pointed to their backs. They had bags over their heads, but both figures were huge, easily twice as big as the twins!

'Goodness, they are enormous!' gasped Francesca. 'I can't believe it! Vampires!'

'I do wish they would hurry up! I have a bad feeling about this!' Arion moaned.

The executioner put both of the figures in place, he tied the noose around each of their necks, and then at the same time, he pulled away their hoods!

However, instead of seeing grotesque, mutated horrors, like the twins thought they would, they saw two ordinary people, *like you or me!*

One was a man, he had long black hair down to his shoulders and his skin was extremely pale, almost the colour of snow. His black robes were huge, they dragged behind him, soaked in mud.

The other vampire was a girl, she had the same kind of skin as the male, but her hair was brilliantly red, and came down her shoulders in waves and curls.

There were only two things that separated the vampires from normal folk. *Their eyes weren't like yours or mine, they were pitch black, like glassy orbs sitting in their heads. The other was their huge protruding teeth, extremely sharp and terrifying.*

The crowd gasped at the sight, children cried and ran away and even the executioner took a step back.

'Filthy Vampire!' someone in the crowd screamed.

'Yes!' The man-vampire answered bitterly, making the crowd return to silence. 'We are vampires! We have returned from the cursed world, The Vampire King will have his revenge!'

The crowd gasped and screamed, all but the twins who had no idea what the vampires were talking about.

*As the author I can tell you that all will be explained very shortly.*

'Kill them!' the crowd started to cry. As the shouting grew louder and louder the pair of vampires started to laugh, they twisted their wrists violently and wriggled free of their bonds. With their hands free they pulled away from the noose and stepped down from the gallows!

The crowd's shouts turned to screams as they realised what was happening, as people started to run away the twins were separated in the confusion, with Francesca being pulled away in the opposite direction of Arion!

The girl-vampire sprinted after the executioner, who had tried to make a run for it. She kicked him to the floor and in a second had her hands around his throat! The male vampire laughed and headed back up to the platform on the gallows. He removed his huge cloak to reveal two enormous black wings, he stretched them high into the air and then flung them downwards with such force, his body was lifted into the air. He flew high above Francesca, who had found shelter next to an old wooden building.

She searched frantically for her brother. When she finally saw him, he was in the open, running away from the vampires! Without thinking Francesca sprinted towards Arion, grabbing him by the hand. She pulled him out of the way as the black wings swooped down over their heads. The twins took shelter beneath the platform of the gallows, at least the vampires couldn't attack them from above, but they needed to leave as soon as possible.

'I told you this was a bad idea!' Arion moaned, 'Oh, I just want to go home!'

'Me too! And we will.' Francesca reassured.
'Come out! Come out!' the female vampire laughed. The winged creatures glided down from above, and landed in the yard where the crowd had been gathered.
They smelt the air, trying to find the twins!
'This is extremely rude!' came a new voice from behind the vampires.
The creatures snapped their heads to the direction of the voice, to see Elrier the Wizard standing boldly behind them.
'You!' they cried. 'You are the reason we are here!' the male shouted.
'Give us the Bulmarion!' the female hissed, opening her jaw wide and threatening him with her huge fangs.
Elrier smiled. 'You shall not have the Bulmarion today. Feel free to try and take it from me.'

'You can do nothing! The Vampire King will awaken, and when he does you shall all be destroyed!'

'Well until then you can leave these people alone, starting with my friends down there.' Elrier pointed towards Francesca and Arion.

'Friends?' the female whispered. 'Your friends shall suffer the same fate as you, the mark of the vampire!'

'No!' Elrier protested, but before he could move, the vampires had spread their wings and bolted high into the air and beyond the clouds.

The twins came out of their hiding place, covered in mud and not in the greatest of moods.

'What are you doing here?' Francesca scoffed as Elrier bounded towards them.

'Let me see your eyes!' he shrieked, ignoring her question.

Arion and his sister stayed still as Elrier seemed to inspect both of them, then he frowned and turned away.

'What's wrong? What's going on?' asked Arion.

'I'm sorry, but you have been given a mark, a mark of a vampire.'

The twins were following Elrier now, down the high street away from the town hall. Elrier's long cloak flapped out behind him and Arion was sure he could see a long sword on his left side.

'We don't understand, we are fine, we don't have a mark on us.' Francesca protested.

'Look at each other's eyes! The mark is in the eyes!'

The twins turned to each other, looking deep into one another's eyes.

The mark was clear, instead of their normal brown eyes, both twins now had piercing green eyes. The colour was almost glowing, it shone brighter than any other feature on their faces.

'What's happening to us? Why have our eyes changed colour?' Arion demanded.

'I will explain everything in a short while. But first I need Bradire.' Elrier was searching for something in his robes, then from his inner pocket he pulled a long wooden stick. This was the wizard's wand, and he lifted it towards the clouds.

The twins were not sure if they could believe what they were seeing, the wand made the sound of a small whistle, and then as if from nowhere, another man stood next to Elrier.

He was of a similar age to the twins, with curly brown hair and like Elrier (and now the twins) he had brilliantly shiny green eyes.

'I kept it safe, just like you ordered.' the new man said.

'Good, good. Hand it over.' Elrier demanded.

From underneath the new man's dark blue cloak, he pulled a crystal ball, around the same size as an orange. It was glowing a deep, dark blue colour. Francesca thought it might have been one of the most beautiful things she had ever seen.

'Now then Arion and Francesca Fitley, let me introduce you to Bradire, my assistant,' Elrier smiled, still holding the crystal globe. 'Bradire and I are going to tell you everything.'

'It's about time somebody did!' Arion exploded. 'What the devil is that thing?'

'This is the Bulmarion, and this is the reason that those nasty vampires were here in the first place. They want it for their master, The Vampire King.'

'Oh goodness, now there is a Vampire *King*?'

'Yes, he's sleeping, but the Bulmarion is keeping him that way, the vampires want to use it to awaken him.' Bradire explained from behind his master.

'There was a war, a very long time ago. Very powerful beings cursed The Vampire King to a never-ending sleep, using the Bulmarion. If it is destroyed, The Vampire King will awaken. Bradire and I are journeying to destroy him before anyone can awaken him.'

The twins looked extremely confused, in fact they *were* extremely confused! This is not the kind of thing they were accustomed to hearing in their small town of Comfort.

Finally Arion broke the silence. 'Well that is all very well and good, but my sister and I must being getting on. We wish you luck

on your adventure and thank you for getting rid of those vampires, but we must be leaving now. Thank you and goodbye!'
As Arion pulled Francesca away, the wizards raced ahead and blocked their path.
'I'm afraid it is far too late for that, I told you, you have been marked.' Elrier said, quite seriously.
Francesca looked into Arion's eyes again, to the brilliant green.
'The mark of the vampires. When a vampire marks you for death, your eyes turn green. Elrier and I are the same, look!'
Arion looked to the wizard's eyes, both of them had the same shade of colour that he could now see in his sister's.
'You have only one choice.' Elrier said solemnly. 'You must come with us. Only Bradire and I can keep you safe now. They will never stop hunting you.'

Arion burst into chuckles of laughter. 'Go with you? That is the most ridiculous thing I have ever heard!'

'That just isn't possible, we have lives in Comfort!' Francesca pleaded.

'The vampires will be back.' Elrier shrugged. 'We must get moving, they wont stop until they have killed us, and released The Vampire King by breaking the Bulmarion.'

The twins argued for quite some time after that, but eventually the prospect of facing the vampires alone overcame the fear of leaving home for more than a week.

The wizards gathered their things, and told the twins that the next step of their journey was going to take them over the mountains and to the world beyond.

Neither of the twins had ever been passed the village of Rundin, their house in Comfort was all they had ever known. As the wizards led the way to the borders of Rundin, the twins took each other's hands, and together crossed the borders and ventured into a world that they had never seen before.

# Chapter 3

## Prisoners of The Watchtower.

After they had left Rundin, the group travelled for many days across fields and forests, towards the great mountains. Arion and Francesca were still not happy about the fact that they had no choice but to go on this adventure, and Arion was very willing to express his anger with every opportunity that he had.

Francesca on the other hand was starting to enjoy the big, wide world. She had always enjoyed walking, and now she was starting to see animals and views that took her breath away.

The Sword of Ralaira.

Rain poured for hours on end, but when the sun shone and the wind was calm there was not much to complain about. She was also starting to enjoy the two wizards company. Elrier had many fascinating stories about his adventures around the world, and Bradire was more than willing to show her magic tricks whenever she wanted. Her favourite trick was when Bradire took a stone from the floor into his palm, closed his fist tight and when he opened it again, the stone had turned into a robin.

It flew away in a hurry, singing merrily as it went.

'Robins are my favourite.' Francesca marveled.

'Then it shall always find you.' Bradire smiled.

Arion had indeed enjoyed the trick, but was determined that he should be angry for the rest of the trip.

*As I have told you, Arion can be very stubborn.*

The twins and the wizards crossed hills and under waterfalls, and at night they camped under the starry sky. Arion and Francesca played their favourite game of how many shooting stars they could see, and every time Arion saw his fifth, he made a wish that he could return home as soon as possible.

The food that Elrier had packed for them had almost gone already. Arion had eaten most of it, while Francesca was happy having as little as possible. She pointed to Arion's ever-growing stomach and laughed, telling him that that was what happened when you eat so much!

One day when the group was walking across a great plain, following the wide mouth of a river, Francesca started to ask more about the dreaded Vampire King and why it was so important that he should be destroyed.

'The Vampire King is easily the most dangerous creature to ever walk on the earth. He is extremely powerful and would spread his evil across every land if he could.' Elrier explained.

'I still don't really understand.' Francesca moaned.

'Thousands of years ago, the city of Ralaira was built. It was so big and so beautiful, that even the gods were jealous. So the evil gods of the underworld sent The Vampire King to destroy it, and kill all good life on this earth. When the Vampire and his armies came, they built the cursed city of

'The Dreadful' next to Ralaira, to taunt the living.' Bradire explained.

'What did the city of Ralaira do?' Arion asked, now intrigued by the story.

'The King of Ralaira, made a sword so powerful that it could destroy The Vampire King himself. The Sword of Ralaira.

A great battle took place, where The Vampire King stole the sword and hid it inside The Dreadful. So the King of Ralaira, with no other way of defeating him, cursed The Vampire King with a never ending sleep.'

'Using the Bulmarion.' Francesca finished.

'Correct.' Bradire smiled.

'So how did you get it? Did you take it from the King of Ralaira?' Arion asked.

'The King gave it to me before he died, he was a good man, and his son James is a good King after him.' Elrier interrupted, before he swiftly moved on and led the group further.

**\*\*\*\***

That night, as the rest of the group slept, Arion heard strange noises coming from the undergrowth around him. Rustling branches and whispering voices getting closer, and closer.

'You are surrounded! Don't try to get your weapons or you will be shot full of arrows.' a voice cried.

The others woke with a startled jump, and Arion hopped to his feet.

'What is going on?' he cried. 'I don't have any weapons!'

'We are but innocent travelers, we wish no one any harm.' Elrier announced clearly.

The bushes around them rustled again, and from the darkness emerged hooded figures, with arrows locked in their bows, pointing at the group.

'These lands are not for travelers, no one crosses these mountains.' the leader said. The rest of the men pulled the twins and the wizards up onto their feet and tied their hands together. Then they started to ransack their belongings. Rummaging through Arion's bag, they pulled out his clothes and his wallet!

'Bring them to the watch tower.' the leader ordered, and with that the group were pulled away towards the hills. Higher and higher their captives took them, until they had to walk in single file, as the path was so narrow. Arion tried not to look at the sheer drop inches away from his feet, but the captives led them even further, and the paths got even narrower. Arion thought if the mountains were any taller, they might be able to see across the whole world! Finally they reached the highest point of the mountain, the path had a magnificent drop on either side now. Far below Francesca could see nothing but cloud. The path led them to a huge gateway, which joined onto a tall wall, which led onto a series of towers that were built onto a very small piece of overhanging cliff. The entire watchtower looked as if it were clinging onto the mountainside by the skin of its bricks.

The group was taken to a small room, there were no windows and no doors. The men who had captured them threw them in and slammed the door shut behind them.

Some time later the door opened again, and in strode a man in brilliant silver armour, a long sword dangled by his side and a long light blue cloak was dragging behind him.

'My name is Paris.' he said 'I am the commander here at the watchtower. You are trespassing. No one can cross these mountains, and so you shall be held here until King James has decided what to do with you.'

'I know King James! He is an old friend of mine!' Elrier insisted, but to no avail. Paris ignored him and closed the door, and then he locked it!

The group had no chance of escaping this tiny room.

'Who is King James?' Francesca asked. The village of Comfort was not part of any kingdoms, and so the prospect of a King confused the twins.

'King James rules over all lands west of these mountains, Paris must be working for him. It will be a long time before word of us can reach James. He lives in the great city of Ralaira. Very far from here.'

'Oh well that's just fantastic, arrested for being on a journey that I didn't even want to be on!' Arion groaned.

'Oh do be quiet!' Bradire snapped. 'The Broken King will wish Elrier no harm.'

'You should not call him that!' Elrier insisted, crossing over to the corner of the room and taking a seat.

'What do you mean The Broken King?' Arion asked.

'The last time The Vampire King rose to power, James was only a prince. He fought the Vampires and could have beaten them, but The Vampire King cursed James' hand. Since that battle James has been seen as a cripple. He's lucky to have people like Paris who are loyal to him, otherwise I fear some people would have tried to overthrow him a long time ago. People who see themselves as stronger than he, but James has a different kind of strength I think, strength of the heart.' Elrier smiled. 'Well hopefully King James will see fit to release us.' Arion piped up, in a sorry attempt at lifting the mood since his last outcry of despair.

'Well you are wizards, surely you can just magic the door open?' Francesca suggested.

'Well of course!' Elrier laughed. 'But we can't just walk out of the castle in broad daylight, we shall wait for the dead of night.'

The guards had indeed taken a lot of things from the group, but Elrier had sneakily hidden his wand up his sleeve, and so he was very confident they could escape during the night!

'While we are here, we might as well see where we are.' Elrier chuckled.

He drew his wand from his sleeve, and pointed it at the wall. With a small pop, the entire wall seemed to disappear, making the tiny room join into another bigger room, making it much roomier.

'This is very dark!' Arion complained, moving into the darkness of the new room. 'I think we should stay back.' Bradire insisted, pulling Arion away. 'I think this is another prison cell, and who knows what might be inside it.'

Then from the darkness came a terrifying, deep voice. It echoed in the cell, making Arion's knees shake.

'Who is it?' the voice asked. 'Who's there?' Elrier moved slowly, and lifting his wand high, he conjured out of thin air a candle with a small orange flame on top. The flame lit the entire two rooms, bathing them all in orange light, which danced

around them making their shadows
flicker.

The voice was coming from a horrific
figure, chained against the wall. It was a
huge goblin with great, sharp horns
sticking out of its head and tusks
protruding forward from its jaw.

Its skin was a disgusting greeny- brown colour and its nails were long and sharp. The chains clinked and grinded as the goblin knelt forward into the light.

'My goodness, you are Vaguum, the goblin warlord.' Elrier stammered.

'Yes. I am he. I am Vaguum the warlord.' the goblin growled, examining the wizards.

'You are Elrier!'

'Yes I am,' he answered.

'I have been searching for you for so long!' Vaguum lunged forward, trying to break free of his chains. They clanged loudly and rattled fiercely, but did not snap. Arion and Francesca jumped back, fearful of the huge creature.

*I can also tell you, reader, that what Arion and Francesca did not know was that Vaguum was The Vampire King's most fearsome warrior, and in the past had commanded the armies of evil. However, when The Vampire King attacked the city of Ralaira, Vaguum ran away, and so was not frozen by the Bulmarion like his master was. Vaguum has been hunting his enemies and trying to find the Bulmarion ever since, trying to earn his masters forgiveness!*

'I see! You wish to kill me to get back into your master's good books!' Elrier laughed. Vaguum roared and snarled, pulling more and more at his chains.

'I shall destroy you, wizard!' Vaguum screamed. 'The Vampire King shall return!'

'We should go.' Bradire insisted, pulling the twins away.

'I agree.' Elrier smiled wearily.

'Wait! I can see your eyes! You have the mark of the vampire!' Vaguum laughed behind them. 'I am not the only one trying to kill you, little wizard!'

The group backed away from the goblin as he continued to laugh. It was a terrible sound, it almost sounded like he was choking. He spluttered and coughed, spitting onto the stone floor of the prison cell.

Elrier raised his wand, about to close the wall again. When suddenly the entire left side of the prison cell broke apart and shattered, sending rocks and wood flying into both the group and Vaguum.

When the dust had cleared, Elrier, Bradire and the twins got up off of the floor. Vaguum was still laughing, and Arion and Francesca shivered at what they saw next. The two vampires from Rundin were standing on either side of Vaguum, with huge long swords grasped tightly in their hands.

'Kill them for us. Destroy the Bulmarion and set our master free!' they screamed.

'I will!' Vaguum vowed.

Then the vampires lifted their swords and brought them down upon the goblin's chains, which broke and fell to the floor. Vaguum the goblin warlord... was finally free!

# Chapter 4.

## The Fight for the Bulmarion

Paris burst through the door of the cells, his sword held tightly in his grip. The golden handle gleamed brightly in the light from Elrier's candle.

Two more guards joined him, both with similar swords and huge shields, silver with black patterns and pointed edges.

'The goblin must not escape!' Paris yelled, and the two guards by his side leapt forward, shields and swords high in the air.

Vaguum was far too quick for them, and dodged their attacks, knocking them back. Then he thrust his giant hands fiercely under their necks and lifted them towards the ceiling.

Yelping with pain, the two guards were thrown backwards across the prison cell. They crashed into Paris and all three of them fell to the floor with a thud, unconscious.

The vampires giggled with delight, and Vaguum raced towards the wizards!

Elrier raised his wand and with a snap, the cell wall was back were it was originally. Francesca could hear the bang where Vaguum had crashed into the wall that he had not seen, and the echoing roar that erupted from the very angry goblin.

'Quickly! It's time for us to leave!' Elrier cried. He gathered his things and picked up one of the guards swords. Bradire picked up the next two and offered it to Arion, who hastily refused.

'Sword fighting isn't really my thing.' he rejected.

'Hurry up!' Francesca insisted, taking the sword for herself and escaping through the door.

'After them!' Arion heard one of the vampires scream, and then there were repeated bangs on the walls and the cell door where Vaguum had been kept.

The corridors of the watchtower were very complicated and dark, Elrier lit the way with his candle and the others followed, keeping a weary eye out for the creatures that were chasing them.

Eventually Elrier led them through the main gateway where a cart being pulled by two horses was tied to a post.

This was there only chance of escape, Elrier and Arion jumped up onto the horses, and Francesca and Bradire leapt onto the cart.

Guards had started to pour from within the castle, led by Paris *(who had clearly now awoken.)*

'After them! The prisoners cannot escape!' he shouted.

As the soldiers raced towards them, another gateway crashed open from across the yard, and in charged Vaguum and the two vampires, each holding giant swords.

'Kill them! Kill them all!' Vaguum ordered, and the vampires charged head on into the group of soldiers, waving their swords high and swinging them violently.

Paris ran towards the goblin, who swung his sword sideways trying to hit him in the side. Paris dodged the attack and swiftly lifted his sword to bring it down on the creature's head, but Vaguum was also very quick, and ducked out of the way.

'You will not escape!' Paris shouted.

Vaguum laughed his terrible, throaty laugh once more and spat towards the soldier. 'Once I have broken the Bulmarion my master will be free. Then I shall come after you and your Broken King!'

The goblin lunged forwards again, and the clanging sound of the two swords meeting rang in everybody's ears.

Every attack that Vaguum threw at Paris was knocked to the side, then with a quick thrust, he slid his sword across the goblin's chest, making the blood drip freely down his dirty armour.

Vaguum roared in pain and charged again, as the vampires mounted another attack into the line of soldiers. Swords clanged and shields thudded, and more soldiers made their way to the battle from different parts of the tower.

As the battle raged on next to them, the horses pulled the cart away, and with a jolt the group were being towed through the main gateway and back down the mountain.

Behind them, Vaguum had escaped Paris and stolen a different horse, and was now racing to catch up. He chomped his huge teeth and held his sword high.

'Give me the Bulmarion!' he screamed.

The horses pulled the cart further down the mountain, and the road was extremely thin. There was a huge drop on either side of the pathway, leading so far down that they couldn't see the bottom, they could only see clouds. Arion could barely look!

The cart took a sharp turn, making the wheels nearly spin over the side, causing rocks to fall from the edge.

Vaguum was extremely close now, he reached out with his sharp claws and tried to grab Francesca, but she was just out of reach and he fell backwards, barely keeping his balance.

'Faster!' roared Elrier, giving the reigns a slight tug.

The wheels of the cart were nearly falling over the edge, but Elrier could not stop, Vaguum was right behind them, snarling and slobbering.

Then to make matters worse, Paris and his soldiers appeared behind Vaguum, riding huge horses.

'Kill the goblin!' they cried, firing arrows from their huge long bows.

There were so many of them crammed onto the slim road at this moment that the sides of the pathway had started to crumble and fall down the mountainside.

'Hold on!' cried Arion as the cart started to drop off the edge.

'PULL!' cried Elrier, and the horses tried to move forward, but the cart was too heavy!

Vaguum came racing up behind them, raising his sword, laughing at the broken cart and his helpless victims.

The cart shifted again, sliding a little more over the edge, one of the wheels even snapped off and fell out of sight, breaking into tiny pieces as it fell and hit the slopes below.

'Francesca! Climb!' Arion cried.

The twins reached for each other, their fingertips touched for a moment, but then Francesca could feel herself slowly fall away.

The weight of the cart pulled it over the edge, and Francesca and Bradire fell backwards over the cliffside, and out of sight!

## Chapter 5.

## Geor The Foul.

Arion had disappeared and now all that Francesca could see was spinning. The cart rolled over violently as it fell through the air, crashing down the slopes and breaking into pieces.

Bradire fell with Francesca, he tried desperately to cling onto what was left of the cart but it was snapping into fragments and scattering all over the mountainside. As they fell further through the clouds, the thin branches of trees started to appear around them, then the trunks, and then finally Francesca, Bradire and the broken pieces of the wooden cart crashed into the ground with a huge crash.

The ground was soft, (Luckily!) A mixture of mud and pine needles that had gathered into a blanket over many years.

'Are you alright?' Bradire asked, standing and making his way over to Francesca.

'I think so, it's just my wrist,' she answered, holding her hand and wincing at the sharp pain shooting through it. 'I've lost my sword.' she moaned, trying to ignore the aching.

'Then we must go. We must find the others.' Bradire pulled her to her feet and dusted himself off.

'Where are we?' Francesca asked, looking around at the strange landscape.

The few trees that surrounded them were dead and crooked, they loomed over Francesca and Bradire like twisted fingers trying to grab them, and through the misshapen bushes, laid the gaping mouth of a cave.

The air was foggy and thick, and the branches of the trees blotted out the sun, making it much darker than it had been before.

'What's that smell?' Francesca scoffed. 'It's revolting!'

*What Francesca could smell smelt like dead bodies and sewage. The smell was thick and stuck in the back of her throat, making her feel like she was going to throw up.*

'We have visitors!' came a strange voice, from inside the cave. The words echoed out from the darkness and rung in Francesca's ears.

'Let us go and greet them.' the voice growled, deep and rough.

The sound of laughing came from the cave, an evil and merciless laugh, making the hairs on the back of Francesca's neck stand on end.

Bradire raised his sword, standing in front of Francesca.

Something was coming out of the cave towards them, something huge. The ground shook when it took a step, making the branches of the trees creak and crack. Francesca could barely make out what the dark shape was as it reached the cave entrance, but as it got closer, she could see that it was the enormous, monstrous body of a giant insect.

Its legs were long and thin, and gripped the sides of the cave. Its body was huge and black, covered in slime and smaller insects which crawled over its back and head.

It had two horns protruding from its forehead, almost as long as its entire body.

The insects mouth was huge, with slobber oozing downwards uncontrollably and teeth the size of Francesca's head!

'Who dares enter my hollow?' the creature growled.

'We beg your forgiveness mighty creature!' Bradire answered. 'We are lost travellers, we will be on our way.'

With that, he started to drag Francesca away from the cave.

'I don't think so,' the insect smiled. 'It is not often that travellers come down here. Come into my cave and tell me of your voyage.'

More insects had started to emerge from the cave, some much smaller and of different shapes. There were spiders and beetles and flies and maggots, each different sizes and colours but all of them looked incredibly horrible.

'Thank you. But I really think we should be leaving.' Francesca tried to smile, still backing away.

'No, I don't think you will be leaving this hollow. My friends want to say hello.' the largest insect laughed again and dug one of its horns deep into the mud. Then he lifted his head high into the air, showering the hollow in disgusting, thick dirt.

The other creatures laughed with their master, and started to speak themselves, they were chanting!

'Geor! Geor! Geor!' they howled.

*As a reader you may be thinking, but how can insects speak? Well, I can tell you, that these are no ordinary insects. The biggest of the bugs is called Geor the Foul, and he is the largest insect that has ever lived. If anyone (such as Francesca and Bradire) enters his hollow, he snatches them up and eats them whole, sometimes leaving the odd part for the other insects.*

'Come into my cave, let me take you, let me taste you!' Geor leant forward and smiled the most ugly smile. Slobber oozed from his mouth and slime dripped from his nose. Behind his head, buried into his neck and back wiggled fresh larvae, maggots and grubs and worms. As he moved, they fell to the floor and buried themselves into the dirt.

'Let me rip you in to tiny parts!' Geor continued, moving forward with the other insects.

Francesca and Bradire were surrounded, with the horrible bugs getting closer and closer, licking their lips.

'Use magic!' Francesca yelled.

Bradire reached into his cloak, and pulled out his very own wand. Lifting it high over his head, he pointed it sharply at the head of Geor.

The wand whistled and fizzed, and from the tip erupted a red flame, which zoomed through the air and hit Geor directly on his nose.

The enormous creature cried out in pain and his whole body rose upwards. His horns crashed into the trees above, sending branches and logs crashing into the bugs beneath.

The other insects darted away, screaming in fear of the fire. 'Geor! Geor!' they cried. The horns on Geor's head were now covered in red flame, he flung his head this way and that, trying to put himself out. But the flames only spread further; everything he touched started to burn.

'Kill them! Tear them apart!' Geor cried. The bugs that were left turned and ran for Francesca and Bradire, twitching their antennae and snapping their pincers.

'Run! Quickly!' Bradire ordered, and they both darted out of the hollow, with the army of insects and the flame covered Geor following them, screeching and howling as they went.

# Chapter 6.

## The Burning of the Forest.

*For now you must forget about the perils that Francesca and Bradire face, even though an army of insects and an enormous fire is a little hard to forget. But you must focus on Arion and Elrier, for the last time we saw them Arion had just seen his sister fall from a great height, and he does not know if she is even alive!*
*This is what happened to both of them after the cart had fallen over the side of the cliff face.*

'Francesca!' Arion bellowed. But there was no answer from his sister, who had disappeared below.

Vaguum bellowed a harsh laugh at the sight of the cart falling and crashing down the slopes.

Elrier tugged Arion away from the edge. 'We have to go!' he shouted, as Vaguum charged his horse forwards once again.

'What about my sister? I wont leave her!' he resisted.

Arion's horse bolted as the huge goblin came ever closer, taking Arion with it. Elrier followed and together they raced further down the mountain, with Vaguum, the Vampires and Paris chasing them.

As they came to the bottom, they found themselves in thick forest. The ground was thick marsh land and the horses struggled to move through it, which meant that Vaguum started to catch up!

'Cover your ears!' Elrier ordered, and he pointed his wand at a nearby tree, which instantly exploded into tiny pieces, scattering across all of them.

The horses reared and threw every single one of them off, including Arion and Elrier, and then they bolted away through the trees.

Pulling themselves up through the mud, the soldiers raised their swords, as did Vaguum and the Vampires, and then Elrier raised his wand, with Arion safely behind him.

'Well, we have a stand off,' Paris sneered, 'Who shall attack first?'

'If you try to fight Vaguum you will all die. There is no need for anyone to die today,' Elrier answered, lifting the glowing Bulmarion from his robes, 'This is what they want.'

Arion pulled at Elrier's shoulder, 'But if you give it to them they will use it to awaken The Vampire King.'

'I know,' Elrier said, 'But there is no other way. Take the Bulmarion and leave.'

The crystal ball glistened delicately in the palm of his hand, Arion thought it strange how such a beautiful object could do so much damage.

Arion couldn't believe what he was seeing. Was Elrier giving in to the evil?

The wizard stretched out his hand and offered the Bulmarion to the vampire closest to him, who smiled as he walked forwards, baring his bloodstained teeth.

Just then, everything seemed to happen at once. There was a flash of brilliant white light and the vampire reaching for the Bulmarion had flown thirty feet into the air and crashed head first onto the swampy ground.

Then another flash of dazzling light, and Paris and the soldiers had been knocked to the floor with such force that they were left unconscious!

Elrier had cast his spell so quickly, that Arion had hardly seen it!

'Liar!' Vaguum screamed, and he charged forward trying to grab the Bulmarion. His razor sharp claws clipped Elrier's hand in the struggle, and the Bulmarion was flung through the air. Higher and higher it went, and then it fell back to earth like a great eagle diving for its prey. But unlike the eagle, it did not stop just before it hit the ground. The Bulmarion came down hard on a large rock, and shattered!

'No!' Elrier screamed, but there was nothing to be done, the blue light of the crystal ball faded away and all that was left were broken shards of glass. The curse had been broken.

'My master is free!' Vaguum yelled. 'You have lost wizard! This is the end for your world!'

'Finish the wizard!' the second vampire ordered, then it spread its wings and flew high into the air. 'The master will want to see me now that he has awoken! I shall go to The Dreadful and prepare our armies!'

As the vampire vanished high into the clouds, Vaguum turned his head to Elrier and Arion.

'What do we do?' Arion begged, backing away from the immense goblin.

*As the author of this book I can tell you that this was the scariest moment of Arion's life so far, as Vaguum raised his sword above his head, Arion thought beyond no doubt that he was going to die.*

*Obviously he doesn't, and later he will learn that this moment was by far not the most fearful of his life.*

*But back to now, and through the thick trees racing towards Arion, was his sister! She and Bradire had escaped the hollow and were running down the mountain, being followed by the hideous Geor and his army of bugs!*

*I apologise, I appear to be waffling once again, let's get back to the story...*

Geor's horn was still on fire, and as he panicked more and more, he threw his horn around, setting more of the trees ablaze.

'Francesca!' Arion screamed when he saw her. 'I thought you might be dead!'

'Bradire! Thank goodness you're alright!' Elrier elated.

'There's no time for that! Run!' Bradire screamed.

Geor charged into the swamp, knocking Vaguum to the side with immense force and setting the entire clearing on fire. The

insects scattered in fear as the flames
surrounded all of them, and thick smoke
started to make them cough and choke.
'Climb a tree, there might be an escape
route up there!' Bradire ordered, and with
that the group, now finally reunited,
started to climb through the trees,
avoiding the flames wherever they could.
Hopping from tree to tree, they
desperately tried to escape the flames.

Geor and his insects had been lost in the flames below, and the blaze was getting hotter and hotter, but thankfully there was no sign of Vaguum anywhere.
'What are we going to do?' Bradire shouted to the others.

Arion held onto the branch of the closest tree as tightly as he could, with his sister next to him.

They tried to scout out a route ahead, but everywhere was ablaze with the brilliant orange light of the killer flame.

Arion heard a huge snap, and suddenly he and his sister were falling downwards, passed the lower branches towards the floor, but instead of being engulfed in the fire, both of them landed in deep water.

The twins had fallen into a lake beneath the tree canopy through which they were climbing, and the cool water was bliss compared to the blazing heat of the fire.

Arion started to swim upwards, the orange light danced on top of the water, brighter than the light of the sun.

As he got closer to the surface, he felt a cold hand grab his shoulder and pull him downwards!

The hand was very strong and didn't let go, deeper into the darkness it dragged him, further into the blackness of the deep lake.

He couldn't breathe, and he couldn't escape. The orange light of the fire disappeared high above him, and everything was gone.

## Chapter 7.

## In The Presence of Mermaids.

Arion awoke with a gasp, relieved to be able to breathe once more. He was lying on his back staring up at a rocky ceiling, with water dripping through the cracks. He lifted himself to his feet and examined himself. He was dry, but covered in cuts and bruises from the fight with the vampires and the goblin, which thankfully were nowhere to be seen. He then looked to his surroundings. He was in a cave, a very beautiful cave. The rock was a shade of gold and around him were pools of brilliant blue water, and sitting gazing into them, were Francesca, Bradire and Elrier.

'Arion!' they gasped happily, and then they all ran together and embraced.

'What happened? Where is Vaguum? What happened to the fire?' Arion exploded.

'Relax, my dear boy.' Elrier smiled. 'We were fortunate enough to be rescued and brought here.'

'Who rescued us?' Arion smiled, thankful that they were all back together again.

'Come with us.' Francesca smiled, leading him through a small tunnel and into an even bigger cave, with more pools and colourful jewels jutting out from the walls. At the far side of the cavern, there sat a brilliant rocky throne, carved into the wall. Sitting on it, was the most beautiful woman that Arion had ever seen.

The first thing he noticed was her eyes. They were a startling golden colour, much brighter than the golden colour of the caves. Her jet-black hair rolled down her long neck and touched her bare shoulders. Below her collarbone, her skin turned to brilliant silver and blue scales, which continued down her entire body. She had no legs, but a huge, muscular tale, which flicked back and forth in the air. She was a mermaid.

On top of her head sat a golden crown, tall and thin. Jewels were embedded into the sides, jewels very similar to those in the walls of the cave.

Two guards rested next to her, their tales dangling loosely from the rocks on which they were resting. Both of them held enormous tridents, sharp and deadly.

As the group moved forwards, Arion noticed more mermaids starting to emerge from their pools, slowly lifting their heads to see the new strangers who had entered their halls.

Elrier led the group towards the guarded mermaid.

'Arion Fitley, this is Iantho, Queen of the Mermaids.' he bowed before her and gestured for the others to do the same.

'This is amazing,' Francesca beamed, 'Can you believe it Arion? Mermaids do exist!'

'We do, little one.' Iantho laughed. 'You are very lucky that we found you. You have all been marked, the vampires will never stop hunting you, and now neither will Vaguum.'

Iantho's voice was soft, but strong. The very sound of it made the bravest of men's heart flutter.

'He will be gathering more goblins as we speak, luckily he will not be able to follow us down here.' Elrier smiled.

'No, he will not. You are safe here and can rest and recover for however long you choose.' Queen Iantho smiled. 'But be warned, The Bulmarion was broken, and The Vampire King has awoken. He is forming new armies and creating new goblins. Vaguum will be back with more creatures, you must choose your path well to avoid them.'

'Thank you for your hospitality, my Queen.' Bradire smiled. 'We would be grateful for some food, if that is appropriate. We lost all of our things when we were attacked on the mountains.'

The Queen nodded and told them all to get some rest, it was at this point that Arion remembered he had indeed lost all of his things, his wallet and his clothes and even all of his food!

But nothing could dampen his spirits, for before him sat the most beautiful mermaid, and when she smiled at Arion the loss of his belongings seemed like no problem at all.

The Sword of Ralaira.

That night, the group spoke alone next to one of the glistening pools. They swapped stories of what happened after the cart had fallen down the mountainside, and what happened to the Bulmarion and Vaguum.

Elrier expressed his worry over that fact that The Vampire King was now awake, and destroying him would be much more difficult.

'This adventure has brought nothing but pain and misery! I say Francesca and I leave now, before Vaguum can get his hands on us!' Arion said.

'Even if we did leave, we still have the mark of the vampire, and would be hunted forever.' Francesca answered.

'I'm sorry, both of you.' Elrier said sadly.

'It's my fault that you are here, I am sorry I have put you in such danger.'

There was a silence, as Arion and Francesca thought about what Elrier had said.

Then Francesca spoke out. 'Even without the Bulmarion, I say we push on. We cannot let an evil vampire roam free, we must destroy him together.'

Arion stood and joined his sister. 'I'm not happy about it, but wherever Francesca goes, I go.'

Elrier and Bradire smiled, and to his surprise, so did Arion.

'The road ahead has become much more dangerous, I have to warn you, I cannot promise you will be safe.' Elrier stated.

Arion and Francesca nodded. 'We want to come,' they announced together. 'What's the plan?'

'We must get into The Vampire King's lair and find The Sword of Ralaira. Only that will be able to kill him,' Bradire explained.

'I say we rest here two more nights, and then leave for the Kingly Mountains, and then we shall be close.'

The group agreed, and that night fed on fish that had been provided by the mermaids, and explored the caves surrounding them.

Arion and Francesca had never been in a more beautiful place, each inch of every wall glistened with a thousand colours, and the blue pools tasted as sweet as strawberries.

As Arion explored another little cave, he came across the smallest pool he had found yet, looking into it he could see that it was extremely deep. Mermaids darted in and out of view, each had a different coloured tail than the one before and hair as long as their arms!

A mermaid suddenly appeared in the pool in front of Arion, it was Queen Iantho, and she was smiling brightly.

'Hello, Arion.' she said.

'Forgive me, Queen Iantho, I did not mean to intrude.' Arion said, taking another bow and turning on his heels to leave.

'There is nothing to forgive, it is natural to be curious.' she smiled, taking his hand.

Arion blushed at her touch; she pulled him into the pool gently and let him sink. They laughed as bubbles popped out of his shirt and jacket, until only his head remained above the water.

'Hold your breath.' she smiled.

Arion did so, and put his head beneath the water.

What he saw next he would remember until the day he died, it appeared that all the pools above were connected, and underneath lay a huge water filled cave.

The jewels in here were even bigger, and the mermaids swam together so beautifully that it looked like they were dancing in mid air. They swam deep, gathering speed and then they shot to the top all together, twisting and turning. Then they separated and started all over again. Arion had never seen so many colours, every inch of the underwater palace burst with brilliant gold and red, then a shimmer of light shifted them to blues and silvers, and then another, and purples would litter down from the cave ceiling.

As Arion ran out of breath, he and Iantho raised their heads above the water.

'That was amazing!' he cried. 'That was the most amazing thing I have ever seen!'

Iantho laughed and gently stoked the soaking hair aside from Arion's face. They laughed again, and Arion took another breath, and followed Iantho back into the pool.

For the next two nights, Iantho took each of them into the mermaid palace, and each of them was just as amazed as Arion. Francesca and Arion spent most of their time in the pools, and when they were not in the pools they were exploring the caves and listening to the amazing stories that Iantho shared.

This was the happiest that the twins had been since leaving their front door in Comfort, and part of them did not want to leave Iantho and the others, but they knew that they must.

As dawn approached on their final day with the mermaids, the group said goodbye.

As the mermaids retreated to the pools, the group was left alone with Iantho sitting on her throne against the jewel-covered wall.

'I have two questions for you before you leave.' Iantho smiled. 'The first is for the wizards, I wish to ask you

why you chose the twins to accompany you on this journey. Why did you ask Arion and Francesca to go with you?'

The wizards remained silent for a moment, thinking.

Then Bradire was the first to speak. 'Elrier and I would not have made it this far without the twins. I think we knew how important they were, even if they did not realise it themselves.'

Iantho nodded and turned her head to Elrier.

'Arion and Francesca are brave and true. They do not yet realise how special they are. They are our friends, and Bradire is right, we would not have gotten this far without them. When I am afraid, it is the twins who keep me going.' Elrier smiled.

Arion and Francesca had not realised how the wizards had felt about them before this moment, and they both felt a warmth towards the wizards more so than ever before.

'The second is for the twins,' Iantho continued. 'I wish to ask you why you carry on this journey when you know of the perils that lay ahead? Why do you keep going?'

Arion and Francesca thought about their answers, part of them didn't know why, but then they answered in unison.

'Because it's the right thing to do.' they replied.

Iantho smiled as Francesca continued. 'We cannot leave Elrier and Bradire to stop the vampires on their own.'

Iantho nodded, and her gaze fell on Arion, who seemed to be still thinking.

'We might not be able to achieve much, but we just want to help.' he answered with a wobbly voice.

Iantho smiled again. 'Do not fear, I think you can and will achieve great things. You already have the bravery and courage that you seek, now you just need to embrace it.'

Arion smiled and looked his last upon the caves that he had come to love.

As the others left, Iantho took Arion's hand once more and knelt forward to kiss his forehead.

'I hope I will see you again.' Arion whispered.

'I hope so too.' Iantho whispered back, then she slowly let go of his hand and sank back into the pool beneath her, and then she was gone.

Arion stood alone in the colourful cave for a moment, then he whispered goodbye once more and followed the others.

# Chapter 8.

## The Creatures in the Caves.

For many days the group travelled over the Kingly Mountains, and its fields and rivers. Each day they were met with colourful sunrises, sunsets and millions of stars stretching across the sky each night. Night after night they played their favourite game of counting the shooting stars, Francesca giggled as she reached five yet again, and closed her eyes to make a wish. She marveled at the amazing sights around them, as did Arion, but his mind kept on returning to the mermaids and their magical caves.

One day as they ate another meal which had been given to them by the mermaids,

Bradire was teaching the twins how to fight. *(As he often did throughout the journey)* and now the twins were getting quite good.

Elrier watched the others while taking a sip from his water sack. His eyes fell on the path that they had followed, stretching back for miles, and he wondered how far behind Vaguum was.

'Where does our path lead us next?' Arion asked Elrier after his sword training.

Elrier pointed towards a small mountain range ahead of them.

'Just over those hills, there is the land of Ralaira and The Cursed City of The Dreadful, where our journey shall end.'

'We are so close,' Arion smiled. 'Then we can find The Sword of Ralaira and kill The Vampire King.'

'We must be wary, Vaguum will not abandon the hunt, and he will not be far behind us.'

With that, the group decided to pack up their things and carry on with their journey. They hoped to reach the mountains by nightfall, but as the group reached the bottom of the slopes a loud battle horn echoed across the land.

Vaguum the goblin revealed himself from behind a row of nearby trees. He had more armour and a cloak hanging from his shoulders, along with a huge battle hammer that he swung from side to side.

Behind him more monsters emerged from the trees, at least fifty of them!

The goblins had found them! This was an ambush!

Each of them looked different, some were small and fat, others tall and thin. All were different colours and carried different weapons. Some had bows and arrows, others had swords, and some had axes while others had hammers! They all jeered and snarled at the sight of Arion, Francesca and the wizards. They bared their teeth and stomped their feet. Vaguum towered above all of the other goblins, even though some of them were huge!

'The Vampire King must have sent them!' Elrier yelled.

'So now there are more of them?' Arion cried.

'We need to find cover! Run!' Bradire screamed.

'KILL THEM ALL!' Vaguum ordered, signaling the charge. The goblins lifted their weapons and started to sprint towards the group. The goblins were much faster and would catch them in no time, but a group of four could not stand and fight fifty goblins!

Elrier needed to think, and quickly!

The wizards waved their wands, and the floor below them opened into a huge mouth of a cave. It looked to go deep underground, and so Elrier pushed the twins through the entrance.

'We can't just hide!' Bradire resisted.

'We don't have another choice.' Elrier snapped, leading them down the hole and into the darkness.

Bradire took out his wand and conjured another candle out of thin air, the wick started to burn instantly, lighting their way further underground.

'Quickly!' Elrier pushed on. 'Vaguum must be right behind us!'

The group followed the tunnel for what felt like a lifetime, and by this point there was no light apart from the orange glow of the flame from Bradire's candle.

 Their enchanting green eyes beamed like torches, brighter than any other parts of their face.

Francesca thought that the way they shone looked quite beautiful, if not for the reason they had changed to that colour in the first place. It was a constant reminder that they had been marked for death by vampires!

 *They were very far down into the ground, in fact no one had ever been down this tunnel before, and there was a very good reason for this, which you are about to find out!*

The group came to rest in a small cave where the tunnel had started to open out, Bradire sent his candle to the middle so that the group could all see each other.

'What is that?' Francesca whispered.

'Where? Is it Vaguum?' Arion jumped.

'Behind Bradire, It's a very strange creature.' Francesca said, moving forward towards the animal.

Bradire moved to the side, and sure enough, behind him sat the strangest creature any of them had ever seen.

*The cave was very dark and the creature wasn't very well lit by the small light of the candle, but I shall do my best to explain it. It was very tall and very thin, with dark, grey, slimy skin. A small stunted nose was placed in the middle of the face above a huge gaping mouth, which opened with a loud snap!*

*Three layers of razor sharp teeth lined the inside of its mouth, bloodstained and covered in slime. If you have ever seen the inside of a leeches mouth, that is what this looked like!*

The Sword of Ralaira.

*I cannot describe its eyes, because it didn't
have any! Flat, lifeless skin rolled over
where the eyes should have been.*

The Sword of Ralaira.

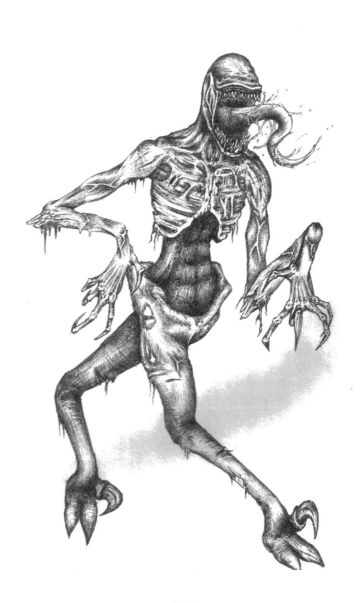

'Perhaps we shouldn't get any closer.'
Elrier whispered, pulling Francesca back.
The creature's head snapped up, and
turned to the direction of the group. They
all stepped back, pressing their backs to
the wall of the cave.
The creature crept forward, its joints
cracking and snapping as it hauled its long
limbs across the floor.
It started to sniff the air, and took one
deep breath in through its nose, and then
another out from it disgusting mouth. Its
chest rattled violently and it coughed up
thick phlegm as it breathed.
As it got closer, the group tried to move
away, but every sound they made only
drew the creature closer. It was only an
arms length away from Francesca, sniffing
at a more fast pace now, like a dog looking
for food.

'What do we do?' Arion whispered, as quietly as he could.

The creature cracked his head towards him, and stretched across the cave with his long arms and legs, pulling himself towards Arion.

The twins could feel the sweat running freely down their faces. Arion closed his eyes, too scared to look as the creature opened it gaping jaws, revealing the disgusting brown and black teeth.

At that moment, Vaguum and his goblins came charging into the tiny cave, they stopped and stared at the creature, which raised its head, took in an almighty breath and let out a long, high pitched howl, like a wolf.

From nowhere hundreds of the bat-like creatures swarmed the group of goblins, biting and scratching and ripping at their flesh.

'RUN!' Arion screamed at the others, and the group darted away from the skirmish, leaving the screaming goblins behind.

'What kind of creatures are they?' Arion breathed.

'I've never seen them before, but I think it's best if we remain extremely quiet and only talk in whispers. They appear to be able to hear even the slightest of sounds.' Elrier insisted.

The others nodded and continued running through the cave.

'Is there any way out of this awful place?' Francesca said, barely making a sound.

'I don't know, all I know is that we cannot go back.' Elrier answered.

They made their way through many miles of caves, each time they thought they may escape to daylight, they came across another hideous creature, sometimes even a group of them. The creatures were huddled in the darkness, and the smallest sound like a footstep made all of their heads turn. They bared their teeth and crept towards the source of the sound. When they were alone once more, the twins turned to Elrier, who buried his head in his hands.

'We are all going to die down here aren't we?' Francesca whimpered.

The wizards said nothing.

'There's no way out.' Arion moaned, wishing desperately for nothing more than to be at home, or at least to be back with the mermaids in their wonderful caves.

'Who is there?' came a familiar voice from the darkness. It was Paris, he emerged into the candlelight, holding a bloodied arm, his head was bleeding and his clothes were torn.

'Paris?' Francesca gasped. 'What happened?'

'I followed you down here, my men and I were going to take you back to The Watchtower. We were attacked by those... things. All of my men are dead.'

'I'm so sorry.' Arion said.

'There is no way out,' Paris stammered. 'Those things are everywhere, I thought I saw Vaguum in the tunnels, but he was being attacked as well, I don't know what happened to him.'

'Quiet!' Bradire ordered, as something else came into the candlelight. It wasn't just one creature, it was close to ten! They weaved through the group, sniffing and dragging their misshapen limbs across the floor.

The group tried desperately to not make a sound, Arion sucked in a breath and closed his eyes, hoping the danger would pass.

A small whimper escaped Francesca's lips and immediately a creature ran to her. It examined the space where the sound had come from, sniffing the air.

It was inches away from Francesca's face, if it moved any closer, they would touch and it would know where she was!

Tears rolled down her cheeks, and sweat ran into her eyes.

The creature breathed heavily, a thick smell of rotting flesh hit Francesca in the face, making her gag.

The creature clicked its teeth, and started to move back, loosing interest in the sound.

The group of creatures started to crawl passed the twins, then the wizards, then Paris, and then the group was alone once more.

'Come with us.' Francesca whispered to Paris.

'Only if you promise not to arrest us again!' Arion spat.

The Sword of Ralaira.

\*\*\*\*

They carried on through the tunnels for
what felt like hours, and it was!

Outside the sun had gone down and then
come back up again before the group
found a way out of the passageways.

The small tunnels opened into a huge,
wide hall. It was so tall that the roof
reached all the way up to the surface, and
through a small opening, the group could
see a tiny slither of sunlight.

'That is how we must escape.' Francesca
whispered happily.

'Finally! Some hope at last!' Arion smiled.

They made their way across the hall until
they were directly beneath the opening.

Then Elrier lifted his wand, and a rope
ladder fell from the roof and landed at
their feet.

'Let's get out of here.' Arion said.

'We must be silent' Elrier reminded them, as he started to climb. Bradire followed him, then Francesca, then Arion and finally Paris.

Higher and higher they climbed, until the floor was hardly visible in the dim light of the candle, which floated upwards with them as they neared the opening high above.

Arion glanced behind him, there was nothing but open space stretching into black.

As they neared the halfway point, Arion felt something dig into his chest. With one hand holding onto the ladder, he reached into his breast pocket and rummaged around. He felt a small metal object that had got caught in his clothes and was now pointing into his chest. He yanked it out and saw that it was his house key, gleaming in the candlelight. He smiled at the thought of home and how nice it would be for him and Francesca to finally return there.

Twisting the key in his fingers, he went to put it back in his pocket, but as his hand neared the inside of his jacket, the key slipped through his fingers and started to fall downwards.

Arion's gasp echoed in the huge empty space of the hall and he thrust his free arm out, trying to catch it. But the key fell silently away from Arion, passed Paris and down into the darkness of the cave.

He closed his eyes, realising his mistake and what was about to happen, he waited for the inevitable clang of metal on stone, and knew that every creature nearby would hear it.

There was only silence as Arion waited, he felt like he had been waiting for hours, his mind pictured the mermaids in their caves again, and the beautiful Iantho...and then... CLANG!!

The metal key hit the stone floor far below, and the sound echoed loudly throughout the cave.

The others stopped climbing and looked about them, confused as to what they had heard.

As the noise continued to echo, an ear-piercing howl erupted below, and within seconds the floor of the cave was overrun with the horrible creatures.

The horde dragged their limbs towards the ladder; their mouths open wide spluttering phlegm and spit.

'Get to the top!' cried Arion as far below the creatures started to climb the ladder, hundreds of them clambered over each other trying to grab the rope and pull themselves up.

Elrier climbed as quickly as he could, and the others followed, holding on as tightly as they could as the ladder shook from side to side.

The creatures were very close, the rope ladder twisted violently and Francesca thought it might snap at any moment. Elrier reached the top, and climbed through the small opening to find himself on the grassland of the mountains. Bradire pulled himself up next, then Francesca and then Arion. The sunlight made their eyes water and the warm air felt like the clean sheets of Arion's comfy bed.

'Help me!' Paris yelled, struggling through the opening.

The creatures were only a meter or so away and they stretched out their long arms trying to grab Paris' legs.

'Pull him out!' Arion yelled, bending to his knees and grasping Paris' arm.

Francesca, Bradire and Elrier helped pull Paris through the hole and to safety, then Bradire pointed his wand at the rope ladder, and it immediately snapped.

The creatures screamed and snarled as they fell downwards into the darkness, then as the last of them disappeared into the black, there was silence.

The sun shone brightly overhead, the wind whistled merrily and the leaves rustled on the trees.

The group was finally safe.

'Thank you,' Paris smiled. 'I was wrong to think you evil.'

'Yes, you were!' retorted Arion.

'You were just doing what you thought was right, Paris. We should not have crossed the mountains, and for that we are sorry.' Elrier said, leading them all away from the opening in the floor. 'What will you do now?'

'I must return to King James, he will want to know why I have left The Watchtower. I will tell him of Vaguum's escape and the threat of The Vampire King.' Paris said.

'Do you think he will help us? King James must have an army, he can use it to defeat the vampires.'

'Perhaps,' Paris frowned. 'He is the King of Ralaira, he will have to march his armies to The Dreadful. I worry more about the doubt his people have in him, will they follow a King who is unable to draw his own sword?'

'That is only a rumour, James is more than capable of leading.' Elrier snapped.

'I know, but I hope he realises that.' Paris grimaced. 'He will be at the castle of The Crossraods, I will go there. Siara will need help.'

'Who is Siara?' Francesca asked.

'The King's sister, she will be in charge of the citadel of Ralaira while the King is away, she will not be expecting an attack from The Dreadful.'

'I hope we will meet you there, and that you can help us.' Francesca smiled.

'I hope that too.' Paris turned away from the group and headed in the opposite direction of the mountain, while Elrier led Bradire, Francesca and Arion around the side of the hill.

The view before them was immense, great rivers and plains sat ahead with the sun bathing them in orange light. In the distance sat two huge castles facing each other, one as beautiful and strong as anything the group had seen, and the other black, decrepit and evil.

'The beautiful city of Ralaira.' Elrier smiled, pointing to the most stunning city.

'And The Dreadful, home of The Vampire King.' Bradire pointed towards the blackened city where smoke rose from the ruins.

'We're nearly there!' Arion smiled. 'We've nearly done it!'

In high spirits, the group headed down the side of the mountain towards the rolling plains of Ralaira, and the two cities.

Elrier thought of the evil monsters he knew they would meet inside The Dreadful, but he also knew that they must find The Sword of Ralaira, whatever the cost.

## Chapter 9.

### The Broken King.

Paris made his way across the countryside, through woods and across fields and plains for many hours. He knew that King James would be staying at The Crossroads Castle, an ancient palace built long ago. *James liked to visit The Crossroad often and when he did, he left Ralaira in the command of his sister Siara, but you can read about her later. Now I will tell you about how Paris knew he must tell James about the threat of The Vampire King.* The path to The Crossroads led Paris down a long ravine, with a river running gently next to the trail.

Paris had always loved the sound of that river and he enjoyed nothing more than looking above him and seeing the trees swaying in the wind high above.

But he could not think about that now.

He continued down the path until he could see the castle of The Crossroads before him.

A guard came forward and Paris announced himself, the soldier nodded and escorted Paris beyond the gates and into the citadel.

The towers reached high and the sun bounced off of the white stone above the hall of the King. The guard knocked politely on the huge oak doors, and then gave a slight push.  They creaked and cracked as they swung open, revealing the small but beautiful hall. Golden patterns ran up the white stone and enormous tapestries hung from the ceiling, and at the head of the hall sat the King on his throne.

'My King.' Paris beamed, bowing before him.

James smiled back, he was of a similar age to Paris, only with more wrinkles under his eyes and long black hair down to his shoulders.

'It's nice to see you again, my friend,' the King answered. 'In these dark times I am glad to see my friends.'

'How so?' Paris asked uneasily.

'More and more people become weary of my ability to rule, most of my own court now call me The Broken King. All because of this.' King James lifted his left hand from under his cloak and removed his glove, revealing the misshapen hand, which had been cursed by The Vampire King so many years ago. The fingers were crooked and bent, the skin was blackened and bloody and the finger nails yellow. James winced as he struggled to flex the fingers.

'The misfortune of your hand does not mean you are unable to rule, you still have a sharp mind and are more than capable of leading your own armies.' Paris smiled.

'Am I?' the King spat. 'There are rumours that I cannot even draw my own sword! And at times I start to believe that myself.'

'I do not believe it.' Paris retorted. 'Many are still loyal to you, and you are the King of Ralaira, a cursed hand does not change that.'

Paris took another step towards the King, and lowered his gaze, his heart started beating more quickly and a bead of sweat ran down the side of his face.

'If I may, my King. We have more troubles than you know. It grieves me to say it, but the Bulmarion has been broken, The Vampire King has returned.'

'That is impossible!' cried James. 'Can it be? How do you know this?'

'I saw it happen, Vaguum the Goblin escaped the watchtower and the forces of evil are gathering. Elrier the wizard and his apprentice are marching on The Dreadful to try and find The Sword of Ralaira, but I fear they will not be enough. The Vampire King is too strong, he will march to the city of Ralaira soon.'

'If what you say is true, Siara is in great danger.' James frowned.

'Ralaira will be attacked first, and then no one will be able to stop the armies of evil.' Paris said.

James sat back in his throne, his eyes scanned the room as he considered his next move. Then he lowered his gaze and a tear rolled down his cheek.

'I have not faced The Vampire King since he cursed my hand. What use will I be now? I cannot fight him with this hand!' James lifted his arm as high as he could, and tried desperately to bend his fingers into a fist, but the pain was too much and the hand fell back to his side limply.

'I believe in you.' Paris urged.

'I know you do.' James smiled. 'It is the rest of the army that I will worry about.'

'You must march to Ralaira at once, my King. We cannot leave your sister Siara to fight alone.'

'I will not leave my sister to face the forces of evil alone, we *will* march to Ralaira.' the King smiled.

'You will face him again, and this time you will win.' Paris said, crossing the room and picking up the King's sword, he jogged up the steps to James' side and offered it to him.

'Could you use your right hand?' Paris suggested.

'I have tried, but I've never been able to fight with my right.' James bit the side of his cheek, and removed the left glove once more. He ran a crooked finger along the edge of the hilt, and grasped it as tightly as he could. Then he slowly started to pulled the sword from its sheath. The sword was heavy, and his hand burned furiously with pain, he tried hard to lift the sword but his hand was too weak. The hilt fell from his fingers and the sword slid back down into the sheath, the handle clanging loudly as it came to a sudden stop.

'The rumours are true!' James yelled. 'I cannot even draw my own sword.'

'No! I do not believe it.' Paris answered, putting the sword down to one side. 'The time is not right, you can do this, you are not weak! You are the King!'

James slumped back into his throne, and slid the glove back onto his hand violently, unable to look at the scars anymore.

'You are a great King, and this proves nothing. When you are faced with your destiny, you will raise that sword high above your head and you will defeat all evils, I know it.'

'I hope you are right.' James whispered. 'But will the soldiers fight with me?'

'They will, my friend.' Paris assured him.

'Then let us ride for Ralaira, I will not abandon my sister. We must get there as quickly as we can. Get the men into marching formation, and ready the horses.'

'It shall be done.' Paris bowed once more, and then left the throne room.

James was left alone. He stood and ran his fingers across the golden patterns of the walls, and wondered if this would be the last time he would see this beautiful place. He decided that it would be. He would surely die in the wars to come, but if that meant he could help his sister, then he knew he must do it.

James often spoke aloud to himself, and as he looked his last upon the beautiful city of The Crossroads, he said goodbye as the sun sank behind the trees, making the air dance with golden light.

'Sometimes when faced with sadness or evil, there is nothing one can do but try to be brave. But how can you be brave when you are faced with losing everything you fear to lose? You can only keep holding on to the hope that love is in the world for a reason.'

# Chapter 10.

## The Cursed City of The Dreadful.

After the weeks of travelling, the attack of the goblins and the creatures in the caves, the group had finally made it to the gates of The Cursed City of The Dreadful.

The immense town was dark, dirty and silent. The walls and buildings were scorched black and the streets were lined with skeletons, old broken siege weapons and spider's webs which were the size of houses.

Elrier led them through the open gates, which reached up high into the sky, as Arion passed under them, it made him dizzy as his head stretched further back while he tried to see the top.

'This is an awful place.' Francesca remarked, tip-toeing her way through the thick layers of dust that covered the floor.

'There's no wind, no birds and no people. Complete silence.' Bradire said.

'Not for long, soon The Vampire King will unleash his armies, we must find the sword before then.' Elrier whispered.

The sun was hidden behind cloud and so a cold shiver spread over the group, the only sound was their tentative steps through the seemingly abandoned city.

The buildings were old and falling apart, high towers knelt to their side, ceilings of great halls had fallen in and the black wood of the houses had started to splinter, and turn to rot.

'This way.' Elrier pointed up the hill to where their path led to the biggest hall of them all.

It was simply huge, the entrance doors where taller than the highest of towers and the spires that littered the roof reached even higher. As they pushed hard on the enormous doors they gave way and creaked open. Dust and bits of rotten wood fell from what was left of the ceiling.

# The Sword of Ralaira.

The group entered the hall of The Vampire King.

'Lets just find the Sword of Ralaira and rid the world of all Vampires!' Arion said.

'It will be in here somewhere.' Elrier answered, and they made their way forward to the head of the hall, where another enormous set of doors sat waiting. This set of doors however had huge bolts across the wood, the biggest set of locks any of them had ever seen.

'Keep your wits about you,' Elrier remarked. 'We're not alone.'

For a moment there was silence, and then a terrifying chuckle of laughter emerged from the darkness.

'You are certainly not alone, wizard.' came a familiar voice.

A shadow moved, and then Vaguum stepped forward, axe in hand, smiling with his horrible blood stained teeth. He had survived the creatures in the caves!

'It's a trap, RUN!' Bradire screamed, but it was too late, the shadows around them leapt into life and Vaguum's gang of goblins had overpowered them in a matter of seconds.

'Take their weapons!' Vaguum ordered, and the others raced forwards, laughing and screeching. They pulled the swords away and reached into Bradire's and Elrier's pockets, and took away their wands!

'You will not use magic to escape again.' one of the goblins jeered.

The group was defenseless, in the firm grip of the goblins; who celebrated loudly and spat at the wizards.

'On your knees!' Vaguum yelled. 'It is time for you to meet your King!'

The other goblins forced the group to the floor, facing the huge, locked black doors that reached into the clouds.

'Face The Vampire King!' the goblins yelled all at once, and instantly the enormous locks on the doors clinked and clanged. They grinded against each other and unlocked by themselves. Then they fell away from the door and crashed at the feet of the wizards and the twins, sending dust high into the air.

Vaguum and the others laughed, still holding the twins on their knees.

'Oh my goodness, it's him! It's The Vampire King!' Francesca breathed. 'He's going to kill us!'

The doors opened, and thick smoke poured forth from the gap. From the darkness beyond the doors a colossal shadow lurked. It moved slowly forwards, revealing itself through the heavy smoke.

The Vampire King stepped forward; his gigantic feet stomped down before the twins, each toe set with long claws like an eagle's talons. He towered over them, his serpent like body twisted high above.

His arms were abnormally long and muscular, claws jutted out from the end of his fingers and a spear-like spike protruded from his elbows.

He sank his head through the thick fog and looked at the twins and the wizards, dropping onto all fours so that he was low enough.

He had an extremely long neck, covered in hard scales and spikes, his head had the shape of a dragons, long spikes lined his snout and his huge jaw was lined with hundreds of razor sharp teeth. He had the eyes of a snake, yellow slits stared at the twins, like great glass orbs on each side of the head.

'I have heard so much about you. Thank you for breaking the Bulmarion and releasing me from my sleep,' The Vampire King whispered. His voice was deep but almost gentle, nothing like Vaguum's horrible, gritty voice. 'Do you wish to kill me?'

The group said nothing, they were all too terrified.

'Vaguum, ensure that these wizards shall never perform magic again.' he ordered.

Vaguum stepped forward with the two wands in his huge palms, and then he grasped them firmly and snapped them in two.

'No!' Elrier yelled in desperation.

Bradire lowered his head, tears falling freely from his eyes.

The Vampire King smiled, and so did Vaguum, who opened his hand and threw the pieces of broken wood onto the floor in front of the wizards.

The goblins all cheered and threw their heads back laughing; The Vampire King paced along in front of the group, a long, wet, forked tongue slipped through the sharp front teeth and tasted the air.

'Who shall I taste first?' the creature smiled. His long neck bent to the side and his yellow eyes fell upon Francesca.

'The girl I have heard so much about, I have been so longing to meet you, Francesca.' The Vampire King rose high and turned, lowering himself again in front of the girl. 'I shall eat you first, and make your brother watch.'

Arion felt his heart pounding as the forked tongue of the Vampire stretched out and slid across his sister's cheek.

She was about to die, and there was only
one thing he could do. He pulled himself
away from the goblin that was holding him
and threw himself at Vaguum who in his
panic, let Francesca go.
'Run Francesca!' Arion yelled.

The Vampire King rose high into the air and roared in anger, thick spit and phlegm erupted from his mouth and fell to the floor.

'I can't leave you!' Francesca yelled.

'Just go!' Elrier yelled. 'Now! Go to Ralaira!' Francesca managed to duck between Vaguum's legs and made for the exit, she sprinted through the great doors and back out into the open.

The Vampire King screeched in frustration and raised his giant hand. He brought it down upon the side of the hall and knocked over the pillars and walls, causing the left side of the building to collapse.

'I will destroy all of you!' the huge creature yelled, and leapt the full length of the hall in pursuit of Francesca.

He stomped down upon the great black doors and pushed against the huge pillars. The entire wall collapsed under the weight of The Vampire King, it crumpled and fell downwards, crashing into the dusty floor bellow!

'Francesca!' yelled Arion, hoping desperately that his sister had not been crushed.

There was no answer to his call, only the sound of broken wood snapping and falling into the dirt.

The Vampire King turned and made his way back across what was left of the hall. Vaguum wrestled Arion back to his knees and held him harshly by the back of his neck, with the huge axe held at his throat. Arion, Bradire and Elrier couldn't believe what they had just seen, was Francesca dead? They cursed and spat at the goblins as they were dragged through a set of doors on the right side of the hall and onto a balcony, where the whole city of The Dreadful was visible.

Arion looked desperately for his sister, but he could not see her. There was only smoke and ruins.

'Your sister will not escape!' The Vampire King growled. 'No one will.'

'Who will you take instead, master?' Vaguum asked with a smile.

There was a long silence, the massive creature paced from Arion, to Bradire and then to Elrier and then back again.

Arion's heart sank as he suddenly realised what Vaguum had meant.

'You don't need to kill any of us! You have already won!' he blurted.

The Vampire King turned and faced the three men on their knees. A huge grin spread across his lips, and he pointed to Bradire with a long crooked claw.

Vaguum pushed Arion to the ground out of the way, and kicked Bradire to the edge of the platform, where The Vampire King was waiting.

'NO!' Elrier bellowed. 'Take me instead!'

'Don't do this! Please!' Arion and Elrier struggled forward, trying to reach their friend, but the goblins were holding them too tightly.

Bradire raised his hands in surrender, tears swelled in his eyes and his voice cracked as he spoke.

'It is all right. Death is nothing at all.'

The Vampire King stood side by side with Bradire and placed huge hands on either side of Bradire's head.

'Please! Please don't do this!' Arion screamed helplessly, but he knew the creature would not stop.

He looked into his friend's bright green eyes for the last time.

The Vampire King snapped Bradire's neck without hesitation. Then he stepped to the side and let the lifeless body fall sideways, over the edge of the platform and down into darkness.

There was a long silence; Arion and Elrier fell to the floor, unable to control their cries. They gazed at the space where Bradire had fallen, unable to understand how this could have happened.

He was dead, and there was nothing they could do.

They cried and they screamed, but The Vampire King was not finished yet, he came back from the edge of the platform and stood before Arion and Elrier.

'It is time.' he said.

'Behold our power, behold the wrath of The Vampire King.' Vaguum growled, as he raised his huge battle horn into the air and blew hard.

The horn blast echoed across the entire city, loud and clear.

Arion had to cover his ears from the sound.

As the echoes died away, the city slowly started to move all at once. The ground shook and the walls of the city crumpled, giving way to figures pushing their way out. Goblins of all shapes and sizes emerged from the earth and from inside the walls of the buildings.

The doors of the black citadel opened and legions of goblins marched forward.

Arion and the wizard could not believe what they were seeing; the entire city had come to life. More and more goblins were emerging from out of nowhere and joining the ranks of the marching army. There were thousands of them, more so than Arion could count.

'We march for The Vampire King!' the commander yelled, and the army behind him echoed the chant.

'Rise, my children!' The Vampire King yelled, 'March to Ralaira, kill every man, woman and child!'

The battle horn was blasted again and the entire army turned and marched down the long pathway, as more and more creatures appeared from beneath the dust.

'Fight me now, wizard.' The Vampire King laughed.

The army marched to the loud beat of goblin drums, each step they took made the ground shake. The beat of sword on shield rung loudly in Arion's ears as the goblins started their war chants.

Vaguum grabbed each of them and threw them into a cage on the balcony, the gang of goblins laughed and snarled as they locked them in and threw away the keys.

'There's nothing we can do!' yelled Arion, pulling furiously on the bars of the rusty cage.

'The world will burn!' The Vampire King screamed, then he charged forward, taking his place at the head of the army, leading it beyond the main gates of The Dreadful and towards the city of Ralaira.

# Chapter 11.

## Francesca Prepares for War.

Francesca Fitley had just escaped the grasp of the evil Vampire King and dodged the collapse of the huge doors; they splintered into gigantic pieces and smashed into the floor behind her as she ran.

The main gates of the The Dreadful were still wide open, and so she fled the city, wishing beyond all hope that her brother and the two wizards would also find a way to escape.

She wished she hadn't left Arion, but she knew he sacrificed himself to save her, and there was only one way she could help him now.

She headed for the great city of Ralaira, directly across the plains from The Dreadful.

When she finally reached the gates, they were just as big as those that The Vampire King had been behind.

The barbican was enormous and stretched far beyond what Francesca could comprehend.

As she entered the city, it was even bigger and more full of people than she could ever have imagined.

It looked like it had been built by giants, the spires of the citadel rose higher than the clouds and could barely be seen. The great stone buildings were battle worn but strong as anything, the grey stone shone silver in the sunlight and the flags on top of the walls flapped fiercely in the strong wind.

Villagers and soldiers busied about the streets, going about their daily business and as far as Francesca could see, everything seemed extremely normal.

It appeared that only she knew of the danger that was heading towards the city. She ran through the town towards the citadel, and then was escorted to the main hall, where she was faced with a very tall women, dressed in beautiful golden armour.

'My name is Lady Siara, what brings you to the citadel of Ralaira?'

'My name is Francesca Fitley. My lady forgive me, but I bring terrible news.' Francesca's voice shook, she felt like she could burst into tears at any moment. 'The Vampire King has been awoken, he has an army and he is marching here!'

'It cannot be.' Siara sighed.

'It is true; he has captured my brother and two of our friends. I don't even know if they are still alive.'

Francesca fell to her knees, and tears fell down her cheeks.

Siara stood and came to her side, embracing her in a tight hug.

'We will find your brother.' she said.

'Thank you.' Francesca stood again, trying to smile. 'You are the King's sister aren't you?'

'Yes.' Siara smiled. 'How do you know? You are not from this kingdom.'

'I met Paris, he told me.'

'Paris is a good man, if he trusts you then so do I.'

Siara smiled and turned away, crossing the room to one of her guards.

'Prepare the city for battle!'

Siara and Francesca rode horses through the streets to the front walls of the city, Francesca had been given the strongest of armour and her chest plate gleamed brightly in the sunshine. Siara had also given her a brilliant sword, slightly curved and razor sharp. The hilt was modeled into a majestic Osprey, the wings folded downwards across the blade like the bird was midflight.

On top of the huge walls, the soldiers worked tirelessly sharpening swords, readying the arrows and gathering spears. Huge Ballista had been loaded onto the walls and above the main gate, commanders shouted their orders here, there and everywhere.

Francesca had never been in a fight, she had barely even *seen* a fight before this adventure. But now the well-oiled machine of a city preparing for a siege surrounded her.

The gates of the city were locked and reinforced with logs and large stones. The battalions of soldiers raced by in smart lines with their armour clanging, marching up the steps to the walls and taking their place among the thousands upon the front lines.

Francesca waited alongside Siara in the main courtyard, running her finger along the edge of her new sword.

'Do you like it?' Siara asked.

Francesca remarked at the beauty of the craftsmanship, but then admitted she had never killed before, and although her adventure so far had been full of peril, she had never been so scared.

'I understand.' Siara assured her. 'I hope you do not need to use the sword, but I fear you will. If that time comes I know you will stand brave.'

'Thank you.' Francesca smiled, stroking the side of her horse's huge neck.

Siara shouted orders to the top of the walls and told commanders to take their legions to different parts of the castle, while Francesca stayed mounted on her horse, unsure of what to do next.

'My lady, what about the women and children, should we evacuate?' a young soldier asked Francesca.

'I'm not the person to ask.' she laughed nervously. 'You should ask Siara.'

The soldier stood in silence awkwardly, twiddling his thumbs.

Francesca turned to Siara who was still shouting commands. Then she thought she should do something useful, and she hopped down from her horse.

'Where is the safest place in the city?' she asked.

'The town hall in the citadel, it has strong doors and is well defended.' the soldier replied.

'Gather all of the children and those who cannot fight, take them to the town hall and seal them in.'

'Yes, my lady.'

Francesca and the soldier passed the order to as many people as they could, and then they got to work evacuating the town.

They went from house to house escorting people to the citadel at the top of the hill

'Quickly!' Francesca yelled, 'The Vampire King will be here soon.'

Francesca kept moving through the villages, she wanted to keep herself busy so that she could concentrate on something other than her brother. Her heart ached at the thought of leaving him and the wizards behind, she knew that she was doing more good here, but the sinking feeling in her heart and stomach was unbearable.

Where was Arion now? Was he alright? Every time Francesca thought about him she felt a sharp pain in her chest, she wanted to break down and cry but she pushed on, helping the elderly and the children to safety.

Most of the town's people had made it to the great hall, the room was now filled with people, and there was barely a place to stand.

'Thank you, Francesca.' the soldier smiled.

'It's the least I can do.' she replied.

At that moment, the battle horn of Ralaira sounded from a tower high above them. A deep long note that rang in every ones ears.

'It's time,' the soldier's smile faded, 'We need to get to the front walls.' he turned to the crowd of people in the hall. 'Seal yourselves in and find some weapons.' Then they turned and made their way down the hill to find their horses.

Siara was waiting in the courtyard as Francesca returned and took her place on her new horse.

'Be brave, men!' Siara cried, 'Show no fear!' Francesca felt a great swell of admiration for Siara, who raised her sword high and commanded her armies forward to the walls. The great horse stomped its enormous hooves and charged up the ramparts, with Siara's cloak billowing out behind it. She turned and shouted down to Francesca.

'Come on! For your brother!' she yelled. At that moment Francesca knew that she must go with Siara and face the coming evil, her brother was alive, she could feel it. She knew that they would be together soon, and if The Vampire King was going to try and stop them, she would face him with the bravest of hearts.

She drew her sword and charged her horse forwards up the ramparts to join Siara on the front wall.

She looked to her sides, the army of thousands was marshaled and battle-ready with her.

Then Francesca looked beyond the wall and her heart sank, she trembled at the sight but held her ground.

In the distance the massive gates of The Dreadful had been opened, and an ocean of goblins, orcs and all manners of unnamable creatures had poured forth. Legions upon legions of dark creatures were lined in position facing the walls of Ralaira. Swords, axes and shields waved furiously in the air and the ground-shaking stomp to the beat of the goblin drums made the soldiers of Ralaira shiver.

'Do not be afraid. Do not be afraid.' Francesca whispered to herself. She gripped the Osprey hilted sword a little tighter.

The goblin commanders came forward from the battle lines, shouting orders for the catapults and ladders to be dragged to the walls.

The goblins charged, throwing spears and shooting arrows at the soldiers above. Francesca lept from her horse and took cover behind the stone on the parapets walk, she shouted for others to move out of the way but they could not hear, the noise of the goblins drums covered every other sound.

Below the armies of The Vampire King had surrounded the outer walls of the castle;

there was no escape for Francesca. They pulled enormous long ladders to the walls and threw them up against the sides.

# The Sword of Ralaira.

As the goblins started to climb, the soldiers of Ralaira drew their swords and readied themselves.

Arrows and spears darted through the air over Francesca's head as she looked over the battlements, the army was advancing and more and more ladders were being lined against the parapets.

'Stand firm!' Siara screamed over the deafening roar of the goblin hordes.

Francesca looked left to the flanking tower, it had been completely overrun, and goblins climbed over their ladders and charged into the Ralairan soldiers.

'For Ralaira!' the soldiers yelled, drawing their swords and storming forwards. Francesca summoned her courage and joined them, swinging her sword high.

'Fire the catapults!' an ogre screamed from below, and a second later, colossal chunks of rock soared over the wall and hurtled into the city buildings. Utter chaos ensued as towers and houses collapsed, people screamed as the catapults launched more boulders over into the citadel.

Francesca pushed her way through the madness to the edge of the parapet walk, where the captain of the ballista stood.

'Fire the ballista!' she cried.

He pulled the lever and the mammoth bolt skyrocketed into the front lines of the goblin army, cutting many of them down and blasting others away.

The defense of the city was holding, the lines of ballista caused chaos below but the goblins continued their charge, and continued to fire their catapults.

'Francesca!' the young soldier cried as he was pushed to the floor by a goblin with a great horn protruding from his forehead.

Francesca charged forward and swung her sword, the goblin span round and lifted his hammer, striking hard down upon Francesca's block. She knocked the hammer aside and thrust her sword into the goblins chest. It gurgled and groaned, collapsing to the floor. Then it gave a slight shudder, and then died.

Francesca had never killed anything in her life, the shock only lasted for a moment, but then another group of goblins made their way towards her.

'Charge!' she cried, and the men to her side followed her into the crowd.

Below the army was still advancing, the ogres and orcs slumped lazily to the base of the ladders and started to climb, and the catapults continued to cause madness on the other side of the great wall.

'Smash down the gates!' the commanders bellowed to the others, and a great battering ram was brought forward to the barbican. It was carried up the walkway and the goblins hammered it into the doors. Time and time again the battering ram smashed loudly into the gates, but the locks were too strong.

Through the lines of the gargantuan goblin legions strolled The Vampire King himself, finally arriving at the battle. He made his way to the great doors and swiped at the battering ram, knocking it through the air impatiently.

'Behold my power!' his snake like head rose into the air and he bellowed a deep, earsplitting howl. He raised his clawed hand high into the air and brought it down hard upon the gates. Winds screamed in the air and lightning struck downwards from the clouds directly into the gates of Ralaira. The great doors split into pieces and fell downwards, orange with flame from the lightning strike. Smoke rose high above the barbican as the last of the

beautiful gateway collapsed to the floor,
leaving nothing but dust and ash.

# Chapter 12.

## The Battle of Ralaira.

Francesca, Siara and the soldiers watched helplessly. The armies of evil swept through the main gates and started to burn the city. They cut down the soldiers and pulled the towers to the ground, the city became choked in smoke, and was surely lost.

The Vampire King roared triumphantly as his army teamed into the city like a plague of locusts.

'Protect the gate! Fight them back!' Siara ordered.

The battalion of men in reserve behind the parapets marched down the hill to the oncoming goblins and charged.

Francesca followed, throwing herself into the wall of swords and shields, swinging and slicing with her sword. Goblins fell before her, only to be replaced with five more, but she fought on.

Beyond the gates The Vampire King continued to command the army, he told his officers to send squadrons of goblins to the far east wall and rip it down.

He wanted the main attack to be on the gate, the sooner they took it over the sooner they would win.

He pushed his way through the anarchy to a pile of giant rocks, and wrapped a huge clawed hand around one. Lifting it high above his head, he hurled it far above the fortifications like it was nothing more than a small stone. The rock seemed to hover above the towers, and then it pounded down into the city streets, knocking over soldiers, cracking through stone houses and towers.

Francesca dove out of the way; huge chunks of rock fell from high above and crushed the men at her side.

The enormous boulder rolled to a stop on the other side of the pathway and was finally still.

Francesca was just about to turn and return to the fight, when she noticed that the boulder hadn't stopped moving at all, in fact it seemed to be shuddering. It rolled from side to side and started to break apart. Spiny legs popped outwards from the edge as the entire rock uncurled, revealing a huge scorpion-like creature. It rose its muscular head and unfolded its pincers. Lastly it uncoiled its tail with the sting at the tip, sharp and dripping with thick, gooey venom. The entire body was a light shade of purple, apart from the hard scales on its back, which were the hard texture of the rock it had been curled into. It was beautiful, but very deadly.

'Run!' Francesca screamed. She turned and sprinted across the courtyard as the scorpion pounced after her, snapping its pincers and crunching its fangs.

She pushed through the battle to try and find cover, but before she could react, the scorpion had scuttled up behind her and snatched her up in its titanic pincers.

She screamed in pain as the claws tightened around her, squeezing the air from her lungs and lifting her high into the air. Francesca tried to twist her body around so that she could swipe at the creature with her sword, but it held her too tightly. The pincers squeezed even more and Francesca thought her ribs might break, and then it harshly threw her to the stone floor.

She turned over onto her back and raised her sword towards it. The scorpion backed away and paced around her in a circle, its tail twitching impatiently.

Then with the speed of lightning it thrust its long tail towards her, extending the sting towards her heart.

Francesca swung her sword with as much strength as she could muster, slicing off the sting from the tail and sending it spinning into the smoke filled air.

The creature roared in pain and withdrew into its rocky shell. She seized her chance and climbed onto the creatures back, raising her sword above her head she yelled, 'For Ralaira!'

Then she threw all of her weight onto the sword and aimed it for the creature's head.

The sword pierced through the rocky shell and sliced through the entire skull, breaking the jaw and sending sharp teeth scattering onto the floor.

The scorpion moaned and tilted forwards, throwing Francesca from its back and crashing into the rubble.

It tried to lift a shaking pincer, but was too weak, and its whole body slumped, dead at last.

Francesca pulled herself up, her knees shook and her ribs still hurt.

She pulled her sword from the creature's head and looked about. The battle raged on, the city was burning and crumbling to pieces around her.

'My lady, what can we do?' a soldier asked her.

'We keep fighting, there is nothing else we can do.' she replied.

At that moment, when all hope seemed lost in Francesca's heart, when all courage seemed to have disappeared, Francesca heard the cheers of the soldiers on the walls.

Siara screamed with delight and the warriors by her side jumped with joy, waving the banners of Ralaira high.

Francesca raced back up the stairs onto the rampart walkways and looked out over the walls.

Beyond the immense sea of the goblin army, emerging from the other side of the mountain was another great army, with thousands of Ralairan banners sailing in the gentle breeze.

'It's my brother! It's James!' Siara cried.

'Our King! Our King has come to save us!' the soldiers celebrated.

The goblins stopped the attack, their heads turned to the mountainside, and to the great army. The surge of creatures swarming through the main gates stopped and waited for commands, it was like the tide of the ocean suddenly coming to a halt.

'Prepare for attack!' the goblin commanders screamed.

The legions turned and formed lines facing the advancing army of King James. Subdivisions of orcs and ogres with spears and axes headed to the front, and archers made their way to the back, getting their arrows ready.

The army of King James drew closer, moving like a well-oiled machine. The thousands upon thousands of riders formed the front lines and readied themselves for the charge. James pushed ahead, so that everyone could see him. Paris was by his side; he exchanged looks with James and nodded. He lifted his arm signaling the army to halt, they did so and James was left sticking out ahead of the front line.

'Let The Vampire King come forth and face me, let the King of the dark world show himself.' James shouted.

The goblin army erupted into laughter at the sight of King James, pointing and holding their stomachs.

The Vampire King came forward to the front lines, laughing along with his men.

'The little prince I met so long ago has become a King!' he smiled. 'James, is that really you?'

'It is me, foul creature. This is my city now, you must leave.'

The goblins erupted into another applause of laughter, even The Vampire King laughed.

James' men shifted uncomfortably, their eyes glancing towards their King and his misshapen hand.

'Steady men.' ordered Paris, noticing the worried looks on the warrior's faces.

'Can you see it, my children? The look of fear in his eyes, in all of their eyes. They do not even believe in their own King.'

James' eyes fell to the floor as the goblins started to laugh again, he gritted his teeth and kept his attention focused on The Vampire King.

'Leave my lands, at once.' James ordered, he wanted the goblin army to turn and run away, but he knew in his heart what was about to happen.

'I shall not turn away and flee from the likes of you, boy King!' The Vampire King screamed, 'I defeated you once, I made you The Broken King, Have you forgotten that it was I who cursed your arm?'

'I have not forgotten' James snapped.

'Why should I flee from a Broken King? Why should I listen to a King who does not have the trust of his own men, who cannot even draw his own sword? I will break you again and again!' The Vampire King rose up onto his hind legs and bellowed out triumphantly over the army of men.

The Goblins exploded into more fits of laughter, some even dropped their swords and shields, creasing over in hysterical amusement.

James felt the anger brewing deep inside of him, he thought back to Paris' advice, '*It will happen when the time is right.*'

He clenched his trembling hands and tried to focus, this was the time that Paris had been talking about.

The time was now.

He lifted his cursed hand and brought it across his body, grasping the hilt of his heavy sword. Ignoring the pain, he bent his fingers around it tightly and made sure he had a secure grip.

Then he pulled the sword from its scabbard, lifting it high above his head.

'You did not break me, you will never break me!' James bellowed.

The entirety of the goblin army fell silent, their laughter died out as quickly as red flames in the rain.

The smile faded from The Vampire King's lips and he dropped back down onto all fours.

'Impossible!' cried one of the goblin commanders, pushing past his own men to get away from the front line.

King James lowered the sword and pointed it at The Vampire King. 'Break me now.' he said, smiling as the army of men behind him cheered and screamed his name.

'For the King!' Paris yelled, a cry that was echoed across the entire army.

Whatever doubt there had been in the hearts of some men in King James' army, it had disappeared the moment The Broken King had drawn his sword to challenge The Vampire King.

'Forward men! To Ralaira!' James bellowed, leading the charge forward.

The army behind him cheered in response and charged their cavalry onward, brandishing swords high and firing arrows from their bows.

The tide of horses smashed into the confused goblin ranks and broke the squadrons into pieces, cutting down the goblins in the thousands.

The Sword of Ralaira.

'Turn and fight! Kill them all, you useless dogs!' The Vampire King cried as his commanders fled the battlefield.

The battle spread across all of the Ralairan plains, catapults were ripped down, siege machines were burning and the ocean of King James' armies swept across the goblins like a wave.

More scorpions had hatched and pounced onto the riders, and trolls and ogres pushed back against the strong defense of the flag bearers.

The Vampire King searched the battlefields looking for James, he drew his gargantuan sword and cut down any man who dared to go near him.

James spurred his horse forwards and rode straight towards the terrifying creature.

He threw himself forward and flung his sword to meet The Vampire King's.

'Fear me!' the creature yelled as the two Kings fought hard, trying to stab, cut, punch and kick the other.

'I do not!' James cried. He dodged the vampire's sword, and stabbed him hard in the hand. The Vampire King screamed in agony as James pushed his sword further through, twisting and ripping it up the wrist, before finally pulling it out.

Thick, black blood dribbled down the Vampire's arm and fingers.

'Now you are a Broken King too.' James laughed as the creature struggled to keep hold of his sword.

'Damn you!' he cried, snapping his jaws and flicking his forked tongue.

James held his ground, ignoring the pain in his hand and focusing on keeping hold of his sword.

But even James did not expect to see what happened next. The Vampire King turned and fled, clutching his wounded hand and wrist.

'Coward!' James yelled, not believing his own eyes.

The battle raged on, the vast army of goblins had been broken apart and the organised squadrons and legions were scattered and confused, but James' army was still scarily outnumbered, and the city of Ralaira was still burning. They fought on against all odds, the cavalry had past the front gates of the city and the men fought in the name of their King.

James was no longer a Broken King; he was no longer the King who could not draw his own sword. He was the King who made vampires flee.

****

Arion and Elrier sat in silence; the tears were still strolling down their cheeks. The wind blew gently across the platform, carrying the smell of choking smoke from the burning city of Ralaira across the plains.

Elrier watched the destruction The Vampire King was causing in the distance, unable to escape, unable to help.

Arion hadn't taken his eyes away from the spot where Bradire's body had fallen, he still half expected his friend to climb back up the balcony and smile as if nothing had happened. But there was only the wind, stirring the dust from below.

He closed his eyes and pictured his living room, the warm fire and his armchair.

Then he imagined Iantho, in her beautiful mermaid caves. She stroked the hair away from his eyes, as she had done in the pool.

He opened his eyes and moved to the bars of the cage, and wiped away the tears.

'We have to get out,' he whispered, 'We have to help Francesca.'

'How? How can we fight such evil?' Elrier whimpered, more to himself than to Arion.

'We find The Sword of Ralaira, and we kill The Vampire King, once and for all.'

Arion searched the dusty floor about the cage, trying to find anything that could help them break the locks of the cage. At last he found a rock, and he started to hack at the chains carefully, as Vaguum was still nearby with his gang of goblins.

'Help me.' Arion spat.

Elrier slumped further into the corner, shaking his head.

'This is all my fault,' he whimpered, 'Bradire is dead because of me.'

Arion stopped attacking the cage and looked to his friend. 'No, that is not true.

Bradire knew the risk, and no matter how much this hurts, we have to carry on. That is what he would have wanted.'

Elrier nodded, wiping away his own tears and quietly crawling across to the bars of the cage.

Arion hammered at the locks and the chains, which finally snapped and fell apart, allowing the cage to be opened.

'Quickly, Vaguum and his men will be back soon.' Arion hurried.

The two made their way back into the great hall of The Dreadful and down into the tunnels below, where Elrier said the sword might be hidden.

'It could be anywhere!' Arion said impatiently.

*They made their way through caves and tunnels, little knowing that Vaguum had found the empty cages above and was hunting them in the darkness.*

'What was that?' Elrier whispered, pointing towards a dark tunnel entrance. 'I heard something.'

From the darkness of the tunnel, Vaguum threw himself with all his might towards the wizard, swinging his hammer through the air and hitting Elrier in the face with such force that he knocked him off of his feet.

The goblin roared in victory, laughing at the old man clutching his face on the floor.

'It is time for you to die, old man.' Vaguum stomped down hard on Elrier's ankle, making him scream in agony.

'No!' Arion bellowed, throwing himself upon the goblin's back.

The pair twisted and writhed, punching and kicking each other furiously. Finally Vaguum threw him off at the feet of Elrier, and kicked him hard in the stomach.

The two backed away into the darkness of the passage, where Elrier pulled a lever, dropping a portcullis between them and the goblin.

'No! You will not escape again!' Vaguum cried in frustration.

The rest of the goblin gang joined Vaguum on the other side of the portcullis, weapons drawn and ready.

Vaguum took a flail from another goblin and swung the enormous spiked head into the air.

'Whoever brings me their heads, gets to keep their own.' Vaguum roared. Then he swung the flail hard into the bars of the portcullis. They rattled and shook but did not give way. Vaguum roared in anger and smashed the flail again and again into the portcullis gate.

BANG... BANG... BANG.

'Run!' Arion shouted pulling Elrier with him through the tunnel.

Elrier's ankle was bleeding, he could barely walk. Arion threw his arm over his shoulder and supported his weight as well as he could.

BANG...BANG...

'Keep going!' Arion cried, hoping beyond all hope that the portcullis would hold.

BANG...BANG...BANG!

Vaguum roared behind them, the tunnel was getting even darker, Arion could barely see where they were going.

The goblins cheered and banged on the portcullis impatiently, pulling on the bars with clawed, bloody fingers.

BANG...BANG....

The bars started to snap and give way, Arion could hear the portcullis being wrenched away from the rocky wall.

BANG...BANG...BANG...SNAP!

The portcullis shattered into pieces and the goblins poured through, sprinting through the tunnel with Vaguum leading the way, swinging his flail high.

'Leave me!' Elrier whimpered as the creatures drew closer and closer. 'I cannot move any faster!'

'I will not!' Arion screamed.

The goblins were only metres behind them, Vaguum swung the flail sending the spiked head zooming over Arion and Elrier's head, smashing into the tunnel wall and breaking the stone apart.

The roar of the goblins was deafening and Arion could do nothing but pull Elrier away, but he knew the goblins were moving too fast. He closed his eyes and waited for the killing blow.

Then everything seemed to be spinning. Had it happened? Was he dead?

The air rushed through Arion's hair and he fell to the dusty floor with a crash, alongside Elrier.

'We must have fallen through to lower levels of the caves.' Elrier gasped.

As the dust cleared, Arion stood, there was no sign of Vaguum or of the other goblins. They must have been left in the tunnel above.

*A very lucky escape indeed!*

In the dim light around them, Arion could see old weapons, boxes, clothes and goblin armour. They appeared to be in a small storing cave, where no one had been for years.

'We should keep moving.' Elrier said.

'Wait,' Arion said, 'I see something.'

In the grey and black layers of dust, there was something shiny and silver. It gleamed brightly even though there was hardly any light.

Arion moved the boxes and the flags that covered it. It was a sword, long and sharp. The hilt was huge, golden with diamonds worked into the sides. The blade was beautiful, there was not a scratch to be seen.

'You've done it, Arion. You have found The Sword of Ralaira.' Elrier smiled.

# Chapter 13.

## Behold The End.

Arion led Elrier through the next series of tunnels, desperately trying to find a way out. He held the sword firmly in his grip, the blade still gleaming magically in the darkness.

Elrier's ankle was feeling much better, and he was able to keep up with Arion, but only just.

Finally the tunnel opened and Arion and Elrier found themselves at the main gates of The Dreadful. Blinding light shone into their eyes and bounced from the blade, the golden sun lighting the edge into flame. The scene before them was immense, the city of Ralaira was consumed in orange firestorms, surrounded by an ocean of fighting men, goblins and ogres. Black storm clouds gathered over the city and thunder echoed across the plains.

The power of The Vampire King had been unleashed.

Arion slowly moved forward towards the commotion, his knees were shaking and his heart was pounding. He felt more fear with each step he took, but he did not once even consider turning to run. He forced himself onwards.

'Wait, Arion.' Elrier pulled at his shoulder, spinning him away from the battle.

'This was not what I intended. You cannot go in there, this is not what was supposed to happen.' he said sadly.

'I know, but it did happen and now we have to fix it.' Arion resisted.

'No, I have to fix it. This is not your fight, Arion.'

Arion stood back, shocked at what Elrier had said.

'Yes. Yes, it is. This is everybody's fight. Whether you are fighting for your family, your friends or fighting just to stay alive, this is everybody's fight. I am going in there to help my sister, this is not your decision to make anymore.'

'We cannot stop this.' Elrier whispered.

'Perhaps not, but we can try. We can help. And if this is the end then I refuse to leave my sister to face it alone.'

Elrier pulled Arion in and hugged him.

'You have more bravery than I can ever know. I am so sorry that I led you here.'

'Well I am not,' Arion breathed shakily, 'I am glad to have shared this venture with you. We cannot give in now.'

Elrier nodded. 'You are the kindest and bravest of men.'

Arion thanked him, and together they made their way to the perils of the battle on the Ralairan plains.

'Vaguum is following us!' Elrier roared as they reached the battle.

Arion glanced behind him, Vaguum and his gang of goblins had lept over the ruins of the Dreadful walls and had joined the battle.

'Keep fighting!' Arion encouraged Elrier. A horde of goblins charged towards them, Arion swung the sword of Ralaira, blocking their attacks. He tried to remember what Bradire had taught him in his fighting lessons, block and parry, don't let them get too close.

He thrust the sword into one of the goblins bellies and pushed the body to the floor. Arion had no time to think about the fact that he had just killed a goblin, as many more raced forwards, attacking him.

Elrier had picked up a sword and was hacking at any goblin or ogre that came near him. 'Stay close!' he yelled to Arion. They fought back to back, trying to get closer to the allies. The main gates of Ralaira were in sight, and below the barbican a rally of men had formed, and at the head of the charge was Francesca!

'Fight for your lives!' she screamed.

The rally charged forwards towards Arion, cramming into the raging battle.

'Francesca! I'm here!' Arion yelled.

They found each other amidst the chaos and embraced as tightly as their tired bodies could manage.

'I thought I would never see you again!' Francesca cried, relieved.

Elrier came to their side and gave Francesca a hug.

'I would not be here if not for your your brother.' he smiled.

'Where is Bradire?' Francesca asked.

Arion and Elrier couldn't bring themselves to say it, but the silence was broken by a number of horses coming to their side, with King James and his men riding them.

'James! It is so good to see you!' Elrier cheered.

'It has been a long time.' James smiled, shaking the wizard's hand.

'King James, I have the sword of Ralaira, we can finally destroy The Vampire King!' Arion cried.

'Then let us find that piece of filth and end this war.' James ordered. His hand was throbbing with pain, but he ignored it and tightened his grip on his sword.

He gave the twins and Elrier a horse, and together they charged the battlefield looking for The Vampire King.

Siara had been separated from her men on the plains; she fought through the chaos and slaughtered each creature that she came across.

Finally she heard the faint call of Paris from across the fields. She followed the sounds and at last she could see him in the distance, fighting Vaguum the warlord! Paris dodged Vaguum's attacks but the goblin was too strong and surprisingly fast. He took hold of Paris' arm and knocked the sword from his hand.

Siara charged forwards, trying desperately to reach Paris on time. She pushed through the crowd, with each step seeming more difficult.

Vaguum raised his sword and drove it into Paris' side, twisting it with vicious malice before walking away, leaving Paris on his knees alone.

'NO!' Siara cried, sprinting to him. She knelt by his side, telling him it was going to be alright.

Paris' eyes found hers and he put his head on her shoulders, too weak to move.

'Behold the end.' he faintly sighed in her ear.

Then his body fell away from hers and hit the ground.

Siara was left alone, surrounded by the terrible battle, crying into her hands at the side of her fallen friend.

'Kill The Vampire King!' King James roared, and what was left of his army rallied to his side.

Many of the goblins turned and fled at the sight of The Sword of Ralaira, dropping their weapons and banners.

The Vampire King threw himself at the rallying men, knocking them aside with his massive clawed hands. 'Victory is nearly ours!' James screamed. There was not many left of either army and The Vampire King stood alone with Vaguum.

Arion and James were knocked from their horses and into the mud; they fought The Vampire King as hard as they were able. Their bodies were tired, weak and bruised but still they swung their swords and tackled the horrible monster.

Francesca and Elrier were facing off against Vaguum, he swung his axe as hard as he could, but the pair knocked him back. 'You die here!' Elrier roared.

The Sword of Ralaira.

The goblin laughed and pushed the wizard to the side, attacking Francesca. She blocked his attack with all of her might, sending the axe spinning through the air and into the mud.

Vaguum seemed to be defenceless, he staggered backwards, surprised by Francesca's strength. She moved towards him and pointed her sword towards his chest. Francesca didn't see him pull the knife from a small hidden sheath on his back. The goblin brought the knife upwards, piercing Francesca's armour and stabbing her in the side.

She gasped in shock as she felt the smooth steel slice through her body. She felt no pain, only a shudder of cold. Vaguum withdrew the knife and held it up in celebration, letting the red blood seep from the handle and onto his hand.

Francesca took her chance; throwing all of her weight forwards, she tightened her grip on her sword and pushed it directly into Vaguum's heart.

The great creature roared in pain and blood spluttered from his lips. He fell to the ground, fighting hard as Francesca pushed the sword further in. Vaguum stared at her in disbelief, his breath gurgled in short, staggered gasps like a dying animal. Then his eyes rolled back and the great horned head fell backwards and thumped to the floor.

Vaguum, the goblin warlord was dead.

Francesca fell to the ground and lay next to the great goblin, holding her side where the wound was still bleeding freely.

Elrier came to her; he dropped his sword and examined the wound. He gasped as he knelt in a vast pool of blood.

'You're going to be fine.' he smiled.

The armies of King James continued to push back the goblin hordes from the walls, many more of them fled and hundreds fell to the swords of the horsemen.

But the battle would not be won until The Vampire King was dead.

The King fought alongside the farmer trying to bring the great creature down. Arion wielded the sword of Ralaira like he was born to do it.

The beast struggled to repel their attacks with his wounded hand, he roared and spat and cursed at his attackers. Finally he launched himself at the pair, and snatched them up into his gigantic hands.

Arion and James were carried to the walls of the citadel, where The Vampire King started to climb the great tower of the King.

'I will cast you down!' he roared, throwing Arion and James atop the tower turret. Arion found his feet, and when The Vampire King opened its mighty jaws and brought them down towards him, he thrust the great sword upwards, striking The Vampire King in his throat.

The Sword of Ralaira.

The sword whistled happily beneath the flesh, finally achieving what it was made to do. The clouds swelled in the air and sent beautiful streaks of lighting down, striking the creature in his head and back.

Arion pulled the sword out, the blade seemed to be alight with orange flame for a second, and then it faded away.

The forked tongue slid between the vampire's lips, covered in black blood. He opened his mouth to say something, but it was lost in the gurgles from the throat.

The eyes of The Vampire King closed and his body slowly fell backwards, over the edge of the tower and down into the flames of the ramparts below.

Everything seemed to be silent. The army of the goblins fled at the sight of their dead King, leaving the land of Ralaira forever.

The Cursed City of The Dreadful collapsed in on itself, huge lumps of rock overturned from below, swallowing the city back to the depths of the underworld from where is was created.

The evil of The Vampire King was vanquished.

Far below James' men cheered in victory, the banners of the King rose high into the sky and the horns of Ralaira sounded with joy.

'It is over.' James smiled.

## Chapter 14.

## Into The Stars.

Arion made his way back across the empty battlefield to where his sister lay. Their friends, Elrier, Siara and James, surrounded her.

He came to her side and took hold of her hand.

'This can't happen.' Arion choked on his tears, hardly being able to speak past the lump in his throat.

'It's alright,' Francesca whispered, trying to smile, 'We beat him, we did what we set out to do.'

'But this isn't fair.' he gritted his teeth, squeezing his dying sister's hand.

'No, it isn't.' Francesca stammered, tears rolling down her cheeks.

The blood had dried in a pool on the floor by her side, bandages were tied across her body, but blood had seeped through most of them.

'This can't happen; you're going to live. Please, you have to live.' Arion insisted.

The black clouds above started to break apart, sending sunshine beaming into Francesca's brilliant, enchanting green eyes.

'Look, the sun is shining again,' she croaked. 'Arion, you must carry on.... Don't go back to the way we were, we have seen the world now. You must live to explore and to enjoy.'

She brought Arion's hand to her lips and kissed it gently.

'Farewell, dear brother. Do not fear. I am just stepping into the next chapter. I'm stepping into the stars.'

'But I don't know what I'll be without you.' Arion's voice cracked, and he sobbed with his sister, all the while squeezing her hand. Francesca's body started to shake, her green eyes found Arion's and for a moment they said nothing. Then hers slowly closed.

'I'm here. It's alright, I'm here.' he said softly.

Francesca took her last gentle breath, then her body relaxed back and her head fell to the side, like she was sleeping.

Arion's body shut down, he collapsed to the floor next to his sister, crying into the dirt.

'The sun is shining, Francesca. The sun is shining again.' Arion whimpered.

She did not reply, her body was still, peaceful and silent.

'Please don't leave me.'

Arion held her hand for a long time after she had died, for he didn't want to let go. The entire battlefield was silent, warriors mourned the deaths of their friends, widows wept for their lost husbands, and children cried for their fathers who would not return.

Arion finally lifted Francesca's hand and kissed it gently, before letting go and covering the body with his travelling cloak. He looked his last upon his sister and let the others take her back into the castle. As he walked through the gates he wondered how everything was still carrying on. He had a strange feeling that everything should have stopped, but it hadn't.

The people of Ralaira swarmed the streets repairing the castle,  crying over the dead and celebrating their victory all at the same time.

*Why was everything carrying on?*

Arion walked up the pathway to the citadel, where Francesca's body was taken. He felt numb, numb to the victory of good over evil, numb to everything around him. Nothing mattered, his sister was gone. His amazing sister, whom he had spoken to everyday, lived with and loved, was just gone. He would never speak to her again, he would never see her smile or hear her voice again.

His knees gave way and he collapsed against the walls of the citadel, unable to hold back his tears.

Arion sat there for many hours, feeling invisible to the rest of the city around him. He couldn't move, and he didn't want to.

Finally Elrier arrived and sat by his side. He said nothing for a long time, it was clear he had been crying as well.

'Of all the things I can do in this world, it seems that I can also do nothing. I'm so sorry.' he finally said.

Arion knew what he meant, but did not say anything.

They sat for many hours more in silence, thinking about what had happened. The sun faded and before they knew it the stars were shining above their heads, glistening like diamonds.

Arion counted the shooting stars, like he had done so many times before with his sister. When he reached five he made a wish, a wish that he knew would never come true.

\*\*\*\*

Over the course of many days the city of Ralaira seemed to heal. The walls and the buildings were broken and black, but the fires were out and the survivors had found their loved ones. The city mourned, but it also celebrated the triumph over the evil of The Dreadful.

James took his place on the throne once more and declared the land of Ralaira safe at last. No one ever questioned him again, and in time, his hand grew less painful. No one ever again called him The Broken King.

Francesca was laid to rest on a hillside alongside Paris and a memorial for Bradire, overlooking the entire city, the plains of Ralaira and the lands beyond. In the morning the sun shone over them, too bright for any cloud to cover, and at night the stars bathed them in silver light.

Arion visited his sister many times, laying flowers and talking to her about anything that came to mind. He even counted the stars with her when he stayed after the sunset.

On what he knew must be his final visit, he told her that he was going to do what she had asked him. He was going to live to explore and not just sit at home in the village of Comfort. He was going to do that for her.

Then he told her that he *must* go home, he wanted to be where he knew her the most, he needed time to move on, and then he would return and see her again.

He laid a hand on her grave, the stone had been warmed by the sun and the gentle breeze rustled the golden leaves on a tree nearby.

'I will return.' he smiled. Then he walked away and didn't let his sister see the tears on his face.

**** 

The next day Arion stood with Elrier atop the barbican, looking out over the plains as the sun continued to beam over the grasslands.

'Are you sure you must leave?' Elrier said.

'Yes, I think so,' Arion tried to smile, 'I want to go home; this place is not the place it should be for me. Comfort is where Francesca would be, and so that's where I want to go.'

Elrier nodded and extended his arm, Arion pushed it aside and embraced the wizard.

'Shall I ride with you?' he offered.

Arion shook his head. 'This is a journey I think I need to make alone. What will you do now that you cannot practice magic?'

Elrier contemplated this for a moment, for many days he had felt lost without his wand, but then he smiled at Arion and said,

'There are many forms of magic in this world, not just what a wizard can conjure but how a friend can make you feel, how good can triumph over evil. I do not know what I shall do now, but I think I have a lot of discovering to do.'

'As do I.' Arion answered.

For a moment they looked at each other in a quiet understanding, they shared a look that can only be passed by friends who have faced unimaginable sadness together.

'Thank you, Arion Fitley,' Elrier understood, 'I hope to see you again, my friend.'

'You will.' Arion smiled.

Then Arion turned away and left the wizard on the rampart walkway and made his way to the stables, there he took a horse and left the city of Ralaira.

Elrier waved from the fortifications above, and continued to wave even as Arion was a small dot in the distance. Then he wrapped his travelling cloak a little tighter around his shoulders, and carried on.

****

The journey that the four companions had taken across the entire land, Arion now made alone. He rode his horse back across the mountains, through the burnt forest and past The Watchtower. He rode through the village of Rundin, where the villagers carried on with their lives, the attack of the vampires a mere memory. The platform where Arion had first seen the creatures still stood, and sunlight beamed through the clouds onto it, making it glow.

Arion didn't stop in Rundin, he carried on and crossed the borders of Comfort, and followed the lane through the woods that were so familiar to him. Then, through the trees he could at last see his home.

He dismounted his horse and paced up the pathway, the cobbles beneath his feet exactly the same as he remembered.

He lifted up a plant pot, and below was the spare key to the front door. *If you remember, Arion dropped his original key in the caves and had lost it forever.*

He turned the key in the lock and gently pushed on the wood.

The door creaked open, and the house within was exactly how Arion had left it. The wood sat by the fireplace, the chair sat next to the window with the beautiful view, and the table clothe sat neatly folded on the counter.

Arion collapsed into his armchair, closing his eyes and breathing in the familiar scent of home.

To his left sat the nest of tables, and on top lay Francesca's book and her reading glasses.

He held them up to the sunlight and wiped away the dust from the lenses with his shirt, and then he gently laid them back where he had found them.

The house was peaceful and silent.

A thin layer of dust had gathered on the surfaces over the months that the twins had been away and the flowers tilted to the sides, but everything else was just how he left it.

Arion was home at last.

For many days he tidied the house, trying hard to get back into routine after so long away. Every morning he would make two cups of tea as he had done for so many years, he would drink his in silence, and the other would go cold on the counter. The village of Comfort carried on as it always had. The villagers were happy to see Arion back and asked all about his adventures and where he had been. Arion wept when he told them about Francesca, as did many of the other villagers. The news spread and over the next week, flowers appeared at Arion's doors with letters of condolences.

Each and every one of the neighbours marveled about the brilliant shine in Arion's green eyes, and how they almost looked like glistening jewels. Arion didn't tell them that it was a mark of death from a vampire, if he did they might think he was mad! He lived with that strange eye shine for the rest of his life, but he never once feared it, as he knew that the vampires were all gone now.

Days turned into weeks, and weeks turned into months, and the village of Comfort moved on, leaving Arion alone in his cottage mourning the death of his sister. Arion made his two cups of tea in the morning, and counted the stars at night. Every time he counted five shooting stars, he made the same wish; the wish he knew would never be able to come true.

This was the case for almost two years, but slowly Arion realised he could not stay like this forever. He realised he could not go back to living his old life, because it wasn't there anymore, and that was a good thing. Life was carrying on.

*I can tell you, dearest reader, that the pain of losing someone you love never really goes away. You simply make room for it, and carry on. You will find hope again.*

*Arion came to understand that no matter how much you don't want them to, things change. He accepted this, and was soon able to smile fondly at the happy memories of his twin.*

*Pain, suffering and loss are a part of life, just as much as joy, laughter and hope. It is a road that we all must travel, and only proves that you have a life worth living.*

*Francesca had wanted Arion to live to explore once she had gone, and after two years in Comfort, after his adventure, he was ready to fulfill his promise.*

*Arion had found his hope again.*

On a bright sunny morning, without a cloud in the sky, Arion Fitley packed his things and once again locked the doors of his cottage in Comfort. He left the village behind, waving goodbye to his neighbours and whispering farewell to the woods and the fields and the animals that he had known for many years.

A robin sang merrily above Arion as he passed, and then flitted away into the colourful trees.

Arion took the road back towards the lands of Ralaira, where he could see Elrier, Iantho, James and Siara again.

A surge of excitement filled his stomach as the land opened into beautiful wonder before him. For it was time for Arion Fitley to explore again, to chase dreams and to live.

The best was yet to come.

# The Sword of Ralaira.

The Sword of Ralaira.

The Sword of Ralaira.

## About the Illustrator.

Scott Robert Greenwood is a creative artist and business owner from Manchester. Scott has studied art all of his life. Along with his art design work he also runs the successful fashion brand-Transpire Clothing.

www.TranspireClothing.co.uk

Thank you to the Murphy family for all
your help with my writing.
It is very much appreciated.

The Sword of Ralaira.

The Sword of Ralaira.

Printed in Great Britain
by Amazon

25240614R00142